A Is For Atonement

By Joseph E. Koegler Jr.

Thanks for the help

Joseph E. Koegler Jr.

Authors Note

I had three basic editors to whom I owe a great deal. Ellen Berkowitz Clark, Alberta, Canada: an old girlfriend from my freshmen year in high school over fifty years ago, and who I reconnected with prior to starting the novel. She was instrumental in encouraging me to keep writing, and is one of my greatest supporters. She is a successful writer and was my prime mover. This novel would never have been written without her.

The second, was a greatest surprise, was my elder sister Mary Ann Engel, Hendersonville, NC. I never realized how much her approval meant to me. Relationships and sibling rivalries in a family of six children over seventy years are extremely complex. Her eight pages of corrections and suggestions, as well as her praise of my writing meant a great deal.

My youngest sister, Monica Blaha, Goleta, CA, eleven years my junior and the baby of the family, presented me with the most complete and detailed edit. I had absolutely no idea of the mastery she had in grammar, punctuation, and formatting. I probably would have found my novel in the trash bin of some publisher without her corrections to my manuscript.

There are a few others whose support was instrumental: Nora Walters Duncan, who read my drafts by chapter, as I was writing, and keep pushing me for the next one; and Marcia and James McKnight who put up with my constant doubts, my fragile ego and yet kept the fires burning.

Oh, don't waste your time driving around Ambridge looking for St. Anne's. I made that up and if you every find O'Shaughnessy's Pub, take me with you.

For Robby

Chapter 1

He stirred awake with a start and a numbing headache. He was also conscious of an old familiar feeling of soft warm flesh pressing gently on him. Thoughts of the comfort of his long past commitments started to dissolve in the reality of the dim light starting to come through a window he did not recognize. Opening one eye and then the other, his mind was catching up; the bar from the previous evening, more beers than he should be drinking, in spite of his ulcers. He was on his left side with a woman's arm across his chest and her leg over his at the knee. Slowly he began to extricate himself. His glasses were on the nightstand next to a wine glass. Oh yeah, and wine too. It was all gradually coming back. He focused on the 7-drawer dresser in front of him and was vaguely aware that there was a dresser on the opposite wall as well, thankful that the mirror above it was not within his sight. Before actually sliding gently from the bed he located his clothes on the floor: his boxer shorts closest to the bed, then his socks followed by his T-shirt. He saw half of his shirt sticking out from the partially closed door. Confident that he had enough of his bearings, he slid from the bed and stood silently looking at the body of the woman he had obviously been with. Lily. At least he thought it was Lily, stirring slightly, rolling onto her back. For a moment he watched, relatively pleased. Not bad, he thought; well-toned legs, nice hips, breasts a little larger than he preferred but overall pleasing. She was definitely attractive, not a beauty but respectable. Could have been a lot worse. She was probably between 40 and 50 years old. He vaguely remembered that she also was divorced a few years back.

By now his head was pounding. He slipped his boxers on and as stealthily as possible gathered up his clothes, checking the pockets of his jeans as he went; Wallet, yes. Swiss army knife, yes. Bills, yes. He slid a little clear pillbox that he carried to check its contents. The little blue one was gone. Ah, yes. He picked up his shirt as he quietly opened the door and closing it behind him, slid into the bathroom on his right. He dressed at once, stopping only briefly to glance in the mirror. Not bad, he thought and ran his fingers through his hair smoothing it back, and reached for a hair grabber from the change pocket of his jeans to pull it into a small ponytail. The one he had on was probably still in the bed somewhere. Oh well, a keepsake. He stood over the toilet, lifted the seat and relieved himself. Damn, he thought as he guided the flow. I didn't use a condom. Not a complete disaster. He hadn't used his real name. He started to think about the number of STDs out there but said to himself, "Fuck it." He tucked himself in and headed out of the bathroom.

As he entered the hall, a gentle voice said, "You really should close the bathroom door." Looking to his left. he saw a young girl standing in a doorway ahead of him. She appeared to be between 16 and 20 and was dressed only in a lacey bra and high cut panty. She was more attractive than her mother, more as a factor of age than anything else, with long dark hair, ample but slim build. The first thing he could think of to say was, "I hope we didn't disturb you last night."

"Not at all," she replied. "Judging by the noise my mother made, you seem to have much more stamina than most of her lovers."

"Yeah, well," he replied, "I'll take that as a compliment." As he looked at the girl who appeared to be deliberately tilting her hips toward him, two thoughts occurred to him at once: first, the Viagra is lasting longer than I would have imagined and second, I've got to get out of here. Looking him up and down she asked, "Would you like some breakfast?"

It was abundantly clear what she was planning on serving. "I'm fine, got to go," he said, brushing past her as quickly as he could without looking rattled. He spotted his coat and checked the pockets. Keys, yes. Phone, yes. Sliding his coat on he said, "Church."

"People miss that all the time," she replied.

As he stepped out of the door he looked back and said, "Not the priest."

He more or less remembered the exit door on his right. Went down a flight and a half of stairs and out to the parking lot. There was a light drizzle; the temperature in the low 40's. He was relieved to see his car. He hit the button for the door lock and got in. He started the car, lit a cigarette and took a breath. He was pleased at his last response; just a little tease for her to think about. As he was backing out of the parking space, he looked up and the girl was waving at him. She appeared to have something in her hand, but he didn't care. He was getting out of there as fast as he could. He hoped he recognized the streets to find his way home. As he was about to pull out into the main street a sense of panic gripped him tightly. He threw the car into park and bent over to check the glove compartment; nothing. He checked the center console; there was his empty holster and his silencer but nothing else. He patted down his coat again. His 9mm pistol was missing. He remembered putting it in his jacket pocket before entering the bar and that it was the object the girl was holding.

There was no choice. He had to go back.

When he had parked in the same spot he had just left, he sat for a minute collecting his thoughts, his hand tentatively on the door handle. He looked at the time on the car's clock, 4:35 am. He exited the car and headed for the door to the building expecting to have to ring the apartment to get in. As he approached however he heard the buzz of the entry access. He opened the door and glanced up at the girl grinning in the window. He climbed up the stairs and was not at all surprised to see the apartment door ajar. Some people just don't have a clue he thought and let out a sigh as he opened the door and walked in. She was lying on her back on the sofa and rubbing the barrel of his gun slowly up and down her thigh. Smooth skin, he thought, would have been better if I had come home with her instead of momma.

"You're no fucking priest," she said almost in a whisper. "Fuck me, I'm a lot better than that old hag" she said.

He sighed again, lit yet another cigarette and sat on the edge of the sofa. After a few drags, he gently put the filter tip to her lips. She took a deep drag and slowly exhaled. He put the cigarette out in a can of beer on the coffee table and reached over and undid her front closure bra, sliding it open with both hands, gently caressing her young firm breasts in one move. She arched her back and reached over to his thigh. He eased his left hand slowly down her stomach and took the pistol from her. Leaning heavily over her torso he kissed her breast while using his right hand to grab a throw pillow beside her head. He sat up straight, put the pillow over her face, pressed the pistol hard against the pillow to muffle the sound and put two bullets into her head.

He waited a few seconds to see if the noise had disturbed anyone, stood up and walked as noiselessly as possible to the bedroom and repeated the process. The quick bursts were heavily muffled by the bed pillow. Relatively sure that no one had heard anything; he walked into the bathroom again and took another leak. After a flush, he took a dry wash cloth and proceeded to walk the apartment wiping down anything he may have touched. He pulled the bed sheet up over Lily's head. He thought about the semen he would have left, but upon reflection had no reason to believe that his DNA was on file anywhere. Besides, the sex could be a separate issue from the murders. He went into the kitchen and found a plastic bag. Retracing his earlier steps in reverse, he picked up the shell casings which were still warm, grabbed the beer can and, careful not to lose the butt, poured the stale beer into a plant by the window and put the can in the plastic bag also. He paused for a second looking at the figure of the young girl and went back to the closet just outside of the bathroom and picked up a white sheet. Returning to the living room he shook out the sheet and placed it over the body. He then turned the lights off using the washcloth and put that in the bag as well. Opening the door with his coat sleeve, he checked the hall, stepped out and down the stairs, hit the bar on the exit and stepped back out into the early morning dark.

Fucking assholes, he thought as he settled into his car, placing the plastic bag into a larger one kept in the car for his own trash.

Chapter 2

Wednesday May 2, 2018

The officer guarding the front door to the apartment lifted the yellow 'POLICE ONLY' tape for Detective Michael Davis, nodding his head toward the inside of the apartment. Mike asked him if the staircase had been gone over already.

"Yes and the door too; too many prints to help much and the door to the apartment has been wiped clean on the inside."

"Thanks Frank," he replied. As he stepped inside there was the usual flurry of activity. Lieutenant Jim Doyle came over to greet him.

"Who found them?" Michael asked.

"The super. Some of the girl's friends convinced him to check on her. She hadn't sent or answered any texts for a few days."

"Names?"

"The girl's name is Marissa Collins. Her mom is Lily Carpenter; divorced about 7 years ago. Returned to her maiden name."

"Husband?"

"Sam Collins. We haven't talked to him yet. The medical examiner just finished up about 15 minutes ago. We were waiting on you to transfer the bodies."

"Do we have the names of the friends?"

"Only one so far. The super didn't talk to the other one. They had to be buzzed in by the super. The girls don't seem to be involved. They never entered the apartment. The super lifted the pillow off the girl's face. That's his vomit in the corner. That was enough for him. He sent the girls away and returned to his office to call it in. He wasn't aware of the body in the bedroom."

"This is slightly out of our normal jurisdiction. Why were we called in?"

"Locals don't have the expertise and the County is already stretched thin on other cases. They requested our assistance."

"Thanks Jim; sign of the times. Get your notes to me as soon as possible. Oh, who put the sheet over the body?"

"I assume the perp. It was there when we arrived. Why?"

"Just curious" Michael replied.

Michael walked over to the sofa. It didn't look like rape. Her arms were bent up over her shoulders, hands tucked between the cushion and the arm of the sofa, palms pressed up against the arm of the sofa. No marks on the body itself, but the head...what was left of it. It was easy to understand the super's reaction. There were pieces of skull hanging on to the fabric on the sofa arm, blood trails running down the cushion and splatter on everything between the sofa and the wall. He made a mental note to make sure the medical examiner checked her lips and inside her mouth for DNA. He doubted they would find any. He noticed the depression on the center cushion. The killer sat there he surmised. He looked at the coffee table and noticed a circular ring that looked fresher than the numerous others. It was clearly on top of the others. He walked around the rest of the room. One of the plants had noticeably more moisture than the others.

"Have them double check the coffee table to see what left that ring and find out what was poured into that plant," he said to Doyle. He looked into the kitchen where two techs were lifting prints off every surface.

One of the techs noticed him looking in and said, "The bathroom and door handles had been wiped down. Nothing usable on them."

No, of course, he thought. This guy knows what he's doing. Controlled splatter from the girl. None on him. He glanced into the bathroom, but trusted his crew. If they already checked it he didn't expect to find anything. Just the same he shouted in to Doyle to make sure they snake the drains, adding, "This looks like it's going to be a tough one."

He walked into the bedroom and knew that this was the work of a pro. The bed pillow was not just placed to muffle the sound. It was placed to minimize splatter and shatter the brain stem: Instantaneous death. No chances. One of the CSI people was placing something into an evidence bag.

"What's that?" asked Michael.

"A hair grabber" he answered.

He looked at the body. "Her hair's not long enough to need that. Hmm..."

"Oh, the doc said she had signs of sex shortly before she died. He already took some fluid samples."

Some hope, he thought.

"Thanks again. You can take the bodies. I'll catch up with the doc in the morning."

"Don't know that he'll have anything that soon. This is our third today."

"Any like this?"

"Not even close."

"This gets priority. Let Mack know that I'll be checking with him in the morning."

He turned and almost knocked over a woman who had come up behind him. It was his new rookie partner. Jennifer Palmer. She had been an officer for about 4 years, but only became a detective 7 weeks ago. She was assigned to Davis with the hope that maybe a female would last longer than his previous partners.

"God, this is sickening," She said. "Do you ever get used to this?"

"God had nothing to do with this. And if you ever get used to it, it's time to quit" he replied.

"Sorry I'm late. The kid was sick," she said.

"I've only been here about 15 minutes myself. Anything serious with Meagan?"

"Not really. She picked today to become a lady. Needed to run some items over to her school. Other than that just hand holding and explaining the facts of life" Jen responded.

"No facts of life here" he said. "Is there anything particular you wanted to see? I just released the bodies."

"If there's nothing you need me to see, I'm good," she answered.

There's a lot I wish you didn't have to see he thought. He respected how difficult it must be for her to raise what was now officially a teenage daughter by herself. Her husband had been in the traffic division. One early morning he made what appeared to be a routine stop and took two bullets in the chest and one to the head. It took almost six months for him to die. That was 6 years ago, and she's been a single mother ever since. Came up through the ranks and made detective 2 months ago. They had only been partners for 7 weeks, but he'd met her daughter Meagan. He liked her instantly, much to his surprise. He normally didn't pay much attention to kids.

He wondered why Jennifer hadn't connected with anyone in the last six years. He had certainly noticed her when he was pursuing her husband's killer. He had caught the guy who was now on death row. All his appeals used up. Mike could never understand the judicial system. He had seen it all too often. The person you convicted was not the same person by the time you finally injected him. But Jen, well she was pretty stoic; handled it better then he thought he could. Probably for Meagan's sake he thought. Still she was young, 36, and very pretty, maybe even beautiful; she kept herself in good shape and smart as a whip. He wasn't ready to admit it, but he liked working with her. Professional distance he reminded himself.

"What do you think Michael?" she asked. He really liked that she called him Michael. He got used to Mike at the academy way back in the beginning but before that, at home and in college he was always Michael. That seemed so long ago, so long ago.

"Nothing yet. We'll have to see what the Doc and CSI find. We'll need to interview the girls who found her and the ex. Not much more we can do here. Let's go back to the squad room and lay out a plan of attack. If nothing else, we can finish the reports on the domestic we just closed and get our desks clear. Oh, one thing that you may find of interest, the killer took the time to cover the bodies. He even took a sheet out of the hall closet to cover the girl. I have a bad feeling about this one."

Chapter 3

Michael Davis had come a long way in the last 17 years. He had graduated from Pennsylvania State University, 21 years old, with a BA in Criminal Justice, his 4th major change. Pre-Law, History, Literature, and finally Criminal Justice. At the time he found it ironic that the guy who had just paid for his last year of college by dealing drugs had a degree in Criminal Justice. Thank god they don't drug test for courses. That was the last of the three majors he'd gone thru; 1st History for a year, then Literature and finally Criminal Justice. Pre- Law was not a designated major for academic purposes. After graduation, he wound up at home with his family; mom, dad and two younger siblings. Hanging with high school friends still around.

It got old fast. Bobby, his old best friend, was married with a kid and decent job managing a clothing store at the mall. He'd quit the drugs and booze. All he talked about was his kid and work. Just didn't cut it anymore. The friends he had that were still into the old ways were obviously sliding down a path to oblivion. He almost tripped into the academy by accident. He was the first member of his family to go to college and his parents somehow thought that should have led to instant success. After the annoying questions from his parents, who were so proud of their son with a college diploma, about his plans for the future he had sent in an application to the police academy. Much to his surprise, after only one interview he received the notification of acceptance. It was like a switch had been flipped in his brain. He felt an instantaneous pride at being accepted, of belonging to something; he searched for a word and realized it was purpose.

His classes started in January, three months away, and began with a physical. Panicked, he started cleaning up his act. No Drugs! None, nada, zilch. Agh! This was going to be a tough test of self control. A hair cut! No, not his beautiful long brown head of hair; his beard. All had to go. His head rang with the sound of the admission officer, "Mike, you're a man now. Time to put childish things away." Oh that repeated voice ringing in his ears. What the hell is childish about it? The words swallowed back in his throat. What came out was "Yes sir." That was the beginning of his long tortured struggle between truth and lies, the ability to survive in a culture you didn't really fit into but needed to survive, even thrive in.

With the help of some dieter's tea and a liter of water just before the test, he passed his drug test. And, as it turned out, the hair cut complemented his slightly elongated face with a strong jaw and pronounced cheek bones. His slightly deep set hazel eyes hinted at a mystery behind them. He made a good looking recruit. He hated the uniform, too starched and stiff for his likes, but very complimentary to his slim build.

He often thought about his family. Not as a cop, worried about how they would feel if anything were to happen to him. No, he knew instinctively that they would handle that with stoicism, but more from how conventionally he had grown up. He considered himself a student of history, his first major change in a long line of changes, trying to figure out what the hell he was going to college for, and was surprised at how predictable the path was. His father was a steel mill worker or mill hunk as they were called in the city of steel. He had worked his way up to a foreman at the hot mill of Jones and Laughlin Steel, by the time the mill shut down. He had been one of the lucky ones who had been there long enough to have both a pension and a pretty good severance package. They managed to get by pretty well as the town died around them. Mike and his brother, Martin, found life relatively unchanged. He remembered how he and his brother would go deer hunting with his dad on opening day every year. Martin, was a natural. He took to it so easily and was a dead shot. Martin brought down a healthy six point buck the first time out. Michael, on the other hand was there only for the beer and camaraderie of a few days at the cabin. Now he was the one who carried a gun while Martin carried a missal.

It was a very conventional Catholic family in the truest sense. First son to the military or, in this case, the police force, second son to the ministry, and a strong willed daughter gone wild. All of their names started with J's or M's after the Holy Family: Mark, his father; Mary, his mother; Michael; Martin, the priest; and Joanna, the wayward daughter. or in this case. Sister. All very different personalities. It seemed the only thing they shared was their thick chestnut hair. It was all very 13th century. Martin had entered the Seminary while Michael had just finished his time at the academy. A year later his mother died of breast cancer. Joanna was a freshman in high school at the time. It had been a terrible couple of years. Mary waited too long to go for a physical and the tumor was well developed when it was discovered. She had a double radical mastectomy, but it was too late. The cancer had already metastasized to the lymph and the bone. She died 8 months later, a relief as it ended the extreme pain she was enduring. Mark did not handle it well and Joanna, the only child still at home, bore the brunt of it. Michael remembered the day after the interment, the three of them sharing a joint and intermittently stories and tears for their mother. Mark was a typical father from the sixties. He was the proverbial bread winner while Mary carried the weight of raising the children. Not to say he was a bad father. He attended teacher meetings, school and sporting events. When the boys were old enough, he took them hunting and fishing. He clearly loved his children but, other than the occasional lecture, he didn't really know his children. That was women's work, along with the household chores, church functions, etc. Without Mary, Mark was lost and took to drinking.

Joanna got pregnant in her senior year of high school and married the father of her child, the first of her three husbands, and moved to California. Martin was ordained and went on to become the youth minister at the family parish in their home town. He wound up overseeing the care of Mark until he died of a heart attack about eight years ago. Michael was working undercover at the time, the assignment that turned out to be his ticket to Detective

Chapter 4

Michael was at the coroner's office bright and early the next day.

"What's your rush? These two aren't going anywhere any time soon" said Mack feigning annoyance. In truth, he rather liked Michael. He did not seem to be as jaded as most of the cops he dealt with. He found him to be intense and bright; smart as a whip. He picked up on things that the few of them that even came in person missed. Asked good questions and learned more every time. He had taken the time to learn the jargon of an autopsy and didn't ask stupid questions. More importantly, he seemed to really care about whom these people were, what their lives were like. Mack also knew that Michael started his career in undercover and it had taken a piece of his soul. Mack first met him during the autopsy of the first person he had killed in the line of duty. He saw the sensitive side of Michael as well as the guilt he put upon himself. That was the first of three perps he had taken down. Most cops never even fire a gun in the line of duty. He also saw Michael's inner strength.

"You know as well as I do Mack, the sooner we get answers the better the chance we have of catching the perp" answered Michael.

"Well I haven't had time to do much yet. There was semen in the elder's vaginal cavity. Already sent it to the lab for DNA. The young one had no signs of recent activity, but showed signs of previous activity, unrelated, but numerous and previous. The entry wounds contained fiber from the pillows, but nothing else. The bullets were sent for ballistics. Appear to be 9mm, but they'll send you a report. Looks like the work of a pro. No signs of a struggle, no skin under the nails, no bruising. Placement of the shots assured an instantaneous kill. Haven't had time for an autopsy yet but when I do, I'll send you the stomach contents. May help but I doubt it."

"Do you have the time of death yet?"

"Not definite but it appears to be around Sunday morning between 4:00 and 6:00 a.m." Mack shook his head and smoothed his beard. "Good luck with this one Mike. I have a feeling it's going to be a toughie."

As Michael headed for the door Mack called to him "Hold up a second. Can't believe I didn't mention it first. Senility setting in. The girl, Marissa I believe, had an abortion a while back. Best I can tell about a year ago give or take a month."

"Hum" said Michael. "That adds a whole new potential motive. That would have been a big miss Doc" Michael chided.

"It would have been in the formal report but you're always in such a damn hurry. Time has a very different perspective down here."

"What down here? You're on the second floor Mack. Hope you can find your way home."

Mack just grunted in response but inside he smiled. He always enjoyed the time he got to spend with Michael.

Michael left and headed back to the Squad room. When he finally, got back to the squad room he was pleased to see that Jennifer was already at her desk going over the crime scene report.

"Looks like we have our work cut out for us. Not much to go on. What did Mack say? Did he have the time of death?"

"He thinks it was very early Sunday morning. I practically had to pay Mack to get that much. You know how he hates to speculate."

"I thought it was just cops he hated."

"Ah, Mack's not a bad guy. He just hates foolish questions. And he also doesn't guess. I rather like the old bird. Reminds me of an old owl. He dots his i's and crosses his t's and watches everything going on about him. You have no idea how many crimes he's solved and received no credit for it. He also gave me another piece of the puzzle. Marissa had an abortion about a year ago."

"That adds another person to find. Maybe a disgruntled father who didn't approve, or maybe didn't know and just found out."

"It's probably a dead end but we need to see if we can track it down. Got a preference on where we start?"

"Well I have an address for the husband and a name and address for one of the girls. I guess we start building history, filling holes. You agree?" Jennifer tended to defer to Michael for priorities.

"Yep. You want to drive or shall I do the honors?"

"Your cars a lot nicer than mine, you drive." She said, grabbing her purse and the folder.

It was another rainy day; just enough rain to make driving a nuisance. They got to the car and she threw her purse in the back seat. It struck him funny that women cops had purses. Guys just use their pockets for their personal garbage but women cops almost always carried a purse with thing like their keys, make up, combs and all that stuff. Michael was a strong supporter of the difference between the sexes.

"How's Meagan today?"

"Calmer", she replied. "You couldn't possible understand cramps, blotting and all the accoutrements of being a women" she replied.

Oh yea, he thought; the purse. "Wait a second. I had a sister. I know about these things" he protested with a smile.

"O.K. Mr. expert. Maybe I should have you explain about it to her."

"I surrender. There are things better left to women. It must be hard on you, raising a kid and all. Particular with all the things you see with work. I mean, we've interviewed kids on the street tricking and all who are no older than your daughter. I admire how well you balance it."

"Don't talk too soon. I've a way to go yet. Haven't had to deal with the real rebellion yet. Wait a couple years. High school, boys, cars. Honestly it scares the hell out of me."

"You know we never really talked about it. Do you have help?"Am I snooping? He thought. What am I fishing for? Walk softly boy he said to himself.

"Well my parents live in town, but she's a little too old for baby sitters. It does help with overnights and conferences and such. Are you volunteering?"

"Yea, I be great with a 12 year old or is it 13?"

"13 and don't sell yourself short Michael. I bet you'd do fine. Besides, Meagan likes you."

"Enough about that. I'll get a swelled head. So where do you want to start? The super, the husband or the girl friend?"

"Well the girl will probably be in school. Wouldn't want to pull her out of class. Not yet at least. Better to get more background first. They've already notified the husband. Maybe hit him in his moment of grief. Get a feel for his mental state."

"I agree, but I really don't see him taking out his daughter. What's the address? You have the report in front of you."

"East Liberty, 2130 North Highland, apartment 316."

"Does he have any sort of record?"

"An old spousal abuse, misdemeanor, 2 drunk and disorderly. Nothing really and nothing recent."

"Hardly a professional killer profile. Well we'll see."

About 10 minutes later they exited the car and entered the foyer of the old apartment house.

Chapter 5

Father Martin left the school on his way to the rectory. His thoughts were lost on the miraculous fortune that had befallen St. Anne's. The church itself was an awesome structure, built at the turn of the last century. It was a stone structure modeled after the 14th century style of architecture with flying buttresses supporting the bell tower at the entry and magnificent stained windows depicting the stages of the cross. There was a round stained glass window 20 feet above the altar depicting Jesus with his left hand reaching out and his right hand was across his chest. It had a brilliant red heart just above his gently curved fingers. The church was positioned in such a way that on Sunday morning the sun shone through the heart sending tendrils of red light out toward the congregation.

They still received good attendance at the Friday night novenas. Even with the gradual decay of the town, or maybe because of it, they still maintained a substantial congregation. The rectory was a mere 200 feet across the parking lot. It was a delightful Tudor style with verandas on three sides and French doors opening out to them. It was three stories tall with 20 rooms in all including a drawing room, a parlor and a library on the first floor along with the large dining room, kitchen, reception area and pantry. Two and a ½ baths had been added; 2 on the bedroom floors in 1930 and a ½ bath off the kitchen added in the fifties, right after they built the school. The convent was on the opposite side of the church, also about 200 feet from the church but separated by a stand of evergreens, a couple of benches and some well-worn paths. Behind all this was the school; a white brick structure with 2 floors and a gymnasium at the far end. The whole complex made a large square within a block. From the main street it was perfectly balanced like the altar itself, with two buildings framing the front of the church and the school as a backdrop.

These days, with the Dioceses closing churches and schools, St. Anne's was an anomaly. The main reason for this was an anonymous donor who had graced the church and school with hundreds of thousands in contributions for the last six years and showed no sign of stopping any time soon. The cashier's checks came in various amounts and random dates. The Diocese had gone to great lengths to discover who was behind this to no avail. The checks came from an offshore account that led to a dead end. The parish, on the other hand, was happy to let sleeping dogs lie. Just a gift from God for their good service to this challenged community.

Father Martin reached the rectory and greeted the receptionist. "Good day, Grace. Anything pressing today?"

"No Father," she replied. "How's everything at the school?"

"You probably know Sister Mary Francis better than I do. If anything was amiss, I'd have to wrestle her for control and you know what? I think she'd win. But the kids seem fine. Billy Castle just passed his last test for altar boy. He'll be serving 11:00 mass this Sunday."

"I'm sure he'll be fine, Father."

"Well, I am celebrating that one so if there are any problems, I'll cover them. He'll be fine even if he's not. I wouldn't turn Father James loose on him. We need all the altar boys we can get these days. The world's changing, Grace, and I'm holding on as long as I can."

"Sometimes I think you're the one holding this place together Martin."

"Shush Grace. I print money in the basement. Don't tell anyone. But you know Grace, it's you and the ladies auxiliary that really keep this whole place together. I don't know how we'd do it without you. I shudder to think what would happen to the school if we had to pay the dear Sisters what we pay the lay teachers, as little as that is."

"Speaking of sisters, Father, how is Joanna? You haven't been out to see her in awhile"

"Bloody heathens, she and my brother. I'm still working on bringing them back to the church, but she's fine. You're right though, I need to go and see her and the kids soon. It's so hard to take the time. Looking for a conference or speaking engagement I can book to justify the cost of a trip."

"Oh Father, you don't owe anything to us. You do so much. Everybody knows how dedicated you are. Take some time for yourself for God's sake, if you'll excuse the expression, Martin."

"My mother couldn't have taken better care of me than you Grace. Now I have to go to the library to work on this Sunday's sermon. Who do you think should win? God or Satan?"

"Oh go on now. You and your jokes, bless you Father."

"Stealing my lines again Grace?"

Chapter 6

Ted Collins answered the door after the second knock, stinking of cheap whiskey. He took one look at the badges they displayed and said "Yeah, come in. I knew you'd be coming. It's always the ex-husband, right?" His eyes were burnt charcoal in deep sockets. It was obvious that it was not from the news of his ex-wife's and daughter's deaths. He'd been on the slide since they invented aluminum.

Jennifer had a slight urge to ask to use the bathroom, maybe snoop around a little but after looking around she thought it better to hold it. The sofa was a peeling vinyl, meant, at some point in time, to approximate leather; the floor looked like it had never been introduced to a vacuum cleaner. In general, it was a filthy mess. She could feel the bugs and vermin without actually seeing any. The walls were an off-white graced with random streaks of brown where some form of moisture had hit them leaving remnant tobacco stains to head for the floor. You didn't need blinds to block out the light from the opaque smeared windows.

Michael started. "I'm sorry for your loss, Mr. Collins, but we really have to ask some questions. Is there someplace we can talk??"

Collins waved them in with a feigned bow.

"When exactly were you and your ex divorced?"

"A hundred years ago."

"We can do this downtown if you'd prefer Mr. Collins" said Jennifer, half to let him know this was serious and half from a desire to get out of this hell-hole.

"God no. It was about 7 years ago. Marissa had just turned 8. Bitch threw me out after she falsely accused me of punching on her. I was too drunk to hit the broad side of a barn but you know how it is. Always the guy's fault. They locked me up and it took 3 days to make bail. She dropped the charges and filed for divorce. I was living on the streets, man. Damn broad wouldn't help at all. A buddy from work took me in."

"And what type of work was that?"

"I was a mill hunk at the time. Wasn't everybody back then? Got in right out of high school. My dad worked there and got me in the union; made good money too, before they started garnishing my wages. Lily was my girlfriend and managed to get knocked up her last year in high school. I knew that it was mine. I figured that she had protection or something, but no. I was on the hook. We got married after her graduation. It's what you did back then, right? Damn bitch nagged constantly. Nothing was ever enough for her. You'd think she was raised in a goddamn palace. Her father was a fucking brick layer. Have to admit though, she was a pretty good fuck herself."

"We could do without the profanity Ted," Jennifer jumped in.

"Sorry ma'am. Life ain't been no bed of roses."

Mike kept going. "When was the last time you saw your wife or daughter?"

"Oh Christ, must have been last year when Marissa got into that trouble. Like I had any money to take care of that."

"What kind of trouble was that Ted?"

"Damned kid got knocked up. Chip off the old block. About the same age her mother started doing me, sixteen. She got an abortion. I wanted no part of it. After all it's a kind of killing. It's a sin, right? I wanted no part of it, not like I was in any position to do anything anyway. Lily had to come up with the money herself. I was barely getting by driving a route for Keystone Plumbing. Still with them. Hey does this mean they'll stop taking money from my pay?"

"You have to check with the court on that," said Michael" Do you mind if we check with your employer?"

"Be my guest."

"Do you own a gun Ted?"

"Got a 30-06 for deer hunting. Haven't used the damn thing in years. Fucking... sorry ma'am, licenses are outrageous these days."

"How about a pistol?"

"Hell no. What would I do with one of those?"

"So I take it you weren't close to your daughter then?" said Jennifer, taking the lead from Michael.

"Tried for awhile, but Mary poisoned her against me. We haven't spoken since she got preggers."

"You could have taken visitation rights to the courts," she continued.

"Yeah, like I got money for that. What would I have done with her anyway?"

"OK, Mr. Collins. If we needed to know your whereabouts over the weekend would that be a problem?"

"Hell no. Same bar most of Saturday and Sunday. Watched the Pirates kick St. Louis's ass last Sunday afternoon. Kelso's down the block. Why? Was that when it happened?"

"That's all we need for now, Mister Collins. It would be best if you stayed in town for awhile. If you think of anything that would help, here's my card. Give us a call.

"Damn, and I was going to visit the Queen of England."

"Oh, one more thing. Do you happen to know anyone who could tell us a little more about either your ex-wife's or your daughter's recent activities?" Michael asked.

"Not really. You might talk to her sister. She sticks her nose into everyone's fuc...sorry, business."

"Can you give us a name and address?"

"Yeah, sure, go bother her for awhile."

They got the information on the sister and left. They didn't offer any further condolences or thanks. When they got back in the car Jennifer looked at Michael and said, "Well that was interesting. I think I need a bath." An image of Jennifer in the bath instantly arose in Michael's mind. He shook it off and said "It's pretty obvious he's not involved. She didn't have an insurance policy or anything, did she?"

"Nothing in the notes. We'll have to run the financials but I doubt that she would leave anything to him. We'll have to add the sister to people to talk to."

"It would have been too easy for it to be a simple domestic I guess. What do you think? The super and then the girl before the sister?"

"Sounds about right, Michael."

"What kind of bath?" Michael knew he shouldn't go there but couldn't help it.

"Huh?"

"You said that you needed a bath," said Michael.

"A solitary one Michael. Shame on you."

He didn't need to turn toward her to know she was smiling.

Chapter 7

Next stop was the superintendent. Just stepping in the place raised the hairs on the back of Jennifer's neck. They rang the super from the box to the left of the inside doors.

"Yes?"

"It's detectives Davis and Palmer. Can we have a moment of your time?"

An answer came in the form of a buzz on the door lock. They entered and looked for a sign or some indication of where the office was. The super solved that problem by coming out of a doorway on their right, waving them forward. Michael turned his head slightly to Jen and whispered, "Did you catch his name?" Jen, as always, was prepared.

"Jim Blocker. 10 years on the job. Single. 58. No record."

Mike absolutely loved her efficiency. It seemed like they had been partners seven years, not seven months. "Thanks" he whispered.

"Mr. Blocker," Michael said as he shook the super's hand. Good grip, he thought. Looked me right in the eyes; appears truly shook by the whole thing Michael thought. There is no way this guy's involved. Michael preferred the busy body type. They usually had good information, more details of victims. Mike couldn't picture this guy bugging an apartment. Not the keyhole type. "Mind if we ask a few questions?"

"Course not. Detective Palmer called earlier to say you'd probably be dropping in."

More points for Jen.

"Come on in. Take a seat. I don't think I can be of much help though."

"It's surprising what pops up." Michael knew that to be true. Some of his best leads had come from statements witnesses thought were insignificant. "Was there anything different, strange or unusual about either Ms. Carpenter or Marissa?"

"Well they were both pretty social; particularly Marissa. Don't guess it makes any difference but the kid seemed to have a wild streak. Whenever I ran into her, she appeared to have been high or drinking. Lots of boys coming around. Had to break up a fight or two between young bucks vying for her attention. She was a pretty young thing. Seemed to know it too. There was that thing last month where you guys were called. Well not you, the regular police. They carried one of the guys out in cuffs."

"Do you know what date that was, Jim?" Jennifer asked getting her pad out.

"Last month, around the 15th or 16th, wait, had to be the 16th. I was signing lease papers with the new couple in B10, just below them. I was worried it might scare them off but they didn't seem to notice. Wonder what they're thinking now. This is really bad for business you know. If you could play down the location that would be really great."

"As much as I would like to control the press, don't think I can help you much with that. Sorry," Michael replied. "How about Ms. Carpenter?"

"Sorry. Don't know that I can help much there. She did seem to have a few men over, but they mostly came in the evening. Never saw them coming, just leaving and usually early in the morning. But I didn't know any of them. There was one about two years ago who seemed to come fairly regularly for a couple months but I haven't seen him lately. Other than that, nothing special and I ain't one to judge. Life can get pretty lonely, if you know what I mean. Been known to have evening guests myself if you know what I mean. Not as frequently, but to each their own. No, it was the kid who had the most friends. She was still in high school you know."

"Do you know what school she went to?" this time from Jennifer.

"Appeared to be Northgate. That's the district we're in. Kennedy Elementary, Wilson Middle and Northgate High. Pretty good schools. Helps with rentals."

"And the girls who asked you to check on her, did you know either of them?"

"Only the one by name, but they both were in and out a lot for a few years. In a way I guess you could say that I watched them grow up together."

"Can you give us the name of the girl you did know?"

"Maggie Sanford. I already gave it to the other cops on Wednesday."

"Just confirming details Mr. Blocker. Do you happen to know where she lives?"

"Not a clue, other than that they went to the same school. And please call me Jim."

"Do you live on the premises, Jim?" Jennifer asked.

"Yeah, best part of the job is free rent. But I live in building 2, next one up."

"How about maintenance issues, Jim?" Jennifer seemed to be taking over the interview. That was fine with Michael. He enjoyed listening to her interview people. She had a knack for making one feel comfortable and talking freely.

"Just the usual; hair clogged the drain in the tub, change the filters, switch the batteries in the smoke alarms. Wish they had wired them directly. Most people take the batteries out cause they go off from cooking. But the only one different was the ceiling leaking. The people in D10 left the tub running with the drain closed, but that was about 4 years ago. They moved since."

"Anything unusual about mail or deliveries you noticed?"

"No. If you had asked me last week, I would have told you they were ideal tenants."

"Sorry I have to ask, but were you ever involved with Ms. Carpenter?"

"Hell no. Not to say I wouldn't have been if she showed any interest. Damn good looking woman, but no. The opportunity never came up. I'm actually flattered that you'd ask. Wish I had been, but no."

"Wish you were my super," Jen said. "He's a toad. Never there when you need him."

Jim Blocker smiled. "If they have an opening, you let me know Ms. Palmer. I mean Detective Palmer."

Mike was surprised at how good she was with people. He knew she owned a home and that this was just a way to connect to the super. If she really needed help around the house, he thought to himself, that was a job he might take. Down boy, Michael said to himself. What is wrong with you today? Focus on the case.

Michael took over the interview. "Well if you think of anything else, or see any of the people show up who have been here before, please let us know. I'm sorry you have to deal with all this. Our guys should release the crime scene sometime early next week. We have a great cleanup team but if you have any problems give me a call. I'll do what I can." Mike didn't want to tell him the bill for the cleanup was the apartment's responsibility or how expensive a blood-born pathogen team was.

After a few more thanks and goodbyes they headed for the car.

"Why didn't you just invite him for dinner?" Michael said to Jennifer as they approached the car.

"Ooh! This from the cop who knows every hooker on Liberty Avenue," Jen said.

"Purely business," Mike responded. "Actually, I was impressed. Who was your interrogation instructor?"

"Kelly," she responded. "But I've been watching you. Keep tension to a minimum, keep it comfortable. Make an ally if you can. About right?"

"Nice to see you've been paying attention."

A bell rang in Jennifer's mind. Keep it cool girl. Don't encourage. Keep it professional. "Hey, I'm still a rookie detective. Isn't that what I'm supposed to do, Detective Davis?"

"My, my. Think I'll break out my parka. Feel a chill."

"You know what I mean Michael. Thin ice here. I get it but, I think we proceed with caution. I enjoy being your partner. Let's take some time to just get to know each other."

Wow, Mike thought. Didn't think I was that easy to read. Damn, I think I love this woman and she hit it right on the nose. This could be a major complication in both of our lives. "Don't read too much into my jokes," said Mike, trying to squelch the direction of this conversation. "What do you think? The girlfriend next or call it a day?"

"Well, we need to write up our notes, and to be honest I'm anxious to touch base with Meagan. Calling it a day sounds good to me. I can check with the school in the morning to find a good time to speak with Maggie. If we catch her at school, we may be able to interview the girl who was with her as well. I'll call her parents tonight to see if they wish to attend."

"Sounds good to me."

They headed back to the squad room. Upon arrival, Jen picked up a folder from her desk and called Mike over. "We got the inventory of the apartment from CSI. Full report to follow but they thought this might be important."

"Yeah, copy on my desk too, along with a preliminary from Mack. You take the inventory. I'll take Mack."

It didn't take long for Jennifer to call Michael over. "You've got to see this. I'm glad we didn't talk to the kids yet. We might want to change some of the usual questions."

"Why? What did they find?"

"$1200 in cash for starters. In the daughters lingerie drawer. New 54 inch TV, two Apple smart phones, latest models; extensive and expensive clothes and over twenty pairs of shoes, including Louboutins. Damn, I can't afford those. This was all in Marissa's room. Nothing unusual in the mother's room though."

"Pretty unusual for a 16 year old."

"Seventeen; her birthday was last month. As far as the inventory, the makeup alone was at least one thousand dollars. They estimate over $10,000 in goods, all in Marissa's room. They are working on the phones. Password protected."

"That's very interesting, particularly in connection with Mack's report. DNA is not back yet but the girl's abortion is confirmed, about a year ago, along with indications of frequent sexual activity since. He found muscular distortion in both the vagina and anus; deterioration of the uterine wall, etc. Do you want to hear this?"

"Not particularly. I'll read the full report later. It fits with the money. Damn, this case gets uglier and uglier. Do you think the mother was involved?"

"Can't rule it out, but it doesn't appear so. All the crucial indications of activity were in the kid's room. More likely the mother was unaware. Her indications are pretty normal. Heavy drinking, hard work, normal sex life, although she definitely had sex shortly before death." The rest was pretty much what he thought. Time of death between 5 and 7 am Sunday morning; Marissa shot first and Lily shortly after. Hair sample on the hair grabber found in the bed was male; chestnut brown. He'll have the stomach contents back from the lab on Monday but Mack said, even without them, Lily was drinking heavily Saturday night."

"I'll follow up with the super to see if he knows if she had a regular bar or pub. Should have thought to ask while we were there," Jennifer added.

"Looks like we have some reading tonight and a full day tomorrow," Mike responded.

Chapter 8

Mike had flourished in the police academy. He was different than most of the others in his class. They mostly broke into two stereotypes. Ex-military who were accustomed to taking orders and thought they were born for this, and average folk who idealistically believed they were going to help save the world. Either way, they both ate up the company bait hook, line and sinker. It seemed that Mike was the only one who ever asked why. Too often the answer was, "That's the way we do things." Occasionally the reply was, "How else would it work? Your life depends on following procedure." If Mike suggested any other approach, he would mostly get the response, "That's a good way to get you and your partner killed son."

Michael excelled at hand to hand combat, small arms fire, marksmanship, physical strength and endurance: all the measured attributes. But somehow, he could never get his head around this partner thing. He really couldn't grasp putting his life in someone else's hands, no less having someone depending on him. Looking around the class he didn't see anyone he himself would want to depend on. Oh, they were nice enough guys, and one nice female, but they were pretty much like the friends he had left behind when he left for college or even more like those guys when he came back. Lost in the world, in situations they just fell into. Going about their lives directed by some other hand; a mother or father, wife, boyfriend, or booze, drugs and parties. At first, he realized that that was exactly what had driven him here too, but more and more that gave way to a sense of purpose, a cause célèbre, an image of a future. It must have shown, because he got noticed. First by his peers in class; if something seemed slightly askance, they instinctively glanced at him waiting for his response. Then by his instructors; he was 'independent'. This was a mixed blessing, as he was soon to find out. When the instructors came together to rate the class, which they did weekly, his name was always the first to be addressed.

"How can you be sure he'd follow procedure?"

"Well, you can bet he would know what it was. It would never be because he didn't know what the situation called for by the book."

"Isn't that the problem? He questions procedure. He could deliberately choose not to follow orders, or worse, hesitate, put others in danger."

"Admittedly, he has a mind of his own but it's a good mind. You must see how the others look to him for guidance. He's a born leader."

"But leading where? That's a lot of trust to put in the hands of a cadet. And he's a loner. We've plenty of examples of what that can lead to."

"You wouldn't be thinking about that investigation into excessive training a few years back would you Carl?"

"Damn little pansy brought all that down. Now we just baby sit and pamper. How do you make them men without discipline?" Carl retorted.

"You want to go on the record with that Carl? Almost cost you your job last time."

"I'm just saying that this is a brotherhood. We have to stand tight together. Can't let some loner put chinks in the armor."

Brian Kelly piped in, "Yeah, and what about the women, Carl?"

"You're just trying to get me fired aren't you, Kelly?"

"Well the kid's got my vote. Doesn't hurt to have some independent thinkers around here. Besides he's a great candidate for undercover. He tries to hide it but he has the past for it. He's quick. Knows the right things to say instinctively but you can tell he's bent a few laws in his life."

And so Mike became the top candidate to infiltrate an up and coming gang; a home grown bunch with a growing drug distribution business and a penchant for violence. It seems they were branching out into extortion and had made some inroads with a few of the city's finest; evidence disappearing just before trial, corrupted samples, witnesses recanting testimony, that kind of thing.

That's how Mike came to find himself in the commandant's office being asked to accept an assignment undercover. The idea appealed to Mike for a number of reasons; the independence, no uniform, and most of all he could let his freak flag fly once again. One of the few things he and his brother Martin had in common was their love of the thick mane of chestnut brown hair that they had inherited from their mother. He couldn't help thinking what a dumb reason that was for taking an extremely dangerous assignment, but it still made him smile. He agreed almost at once and was set up with some minor revisions to his history and a job as a bartender in the area patronized by some of the known gang members. Three months of training on everything from bartending to who his handlers were, how to contact them, when to get out; all the basics.

What he hadn't anticipated was that undercover is a form of schizophrenia. The academy daily drove home the themes of clean living but in undercover the street made clear that clean living was the path to the grave. In deep cover it was necessary to adopt the lifestyle of those you were infiltrating. That did not exactly conform to academy or police policy. It took Mike 6 months to even get noticed. He broke up a bar fight and busted a bottle over a guy's head; exactly the type of blow that will call attention to yourself. A couple of weeks later a mid-level dealer and grunt for the gang named Bugsby befriended him. They went out and beat up a small time dealer trying to come up in the world. Afterwards they went to Bugsby's apartment and smoked some, drank even more. A couple of girls were sent over as a reward. One appreciated Mike most of the night. He amused himself with the thought that he was only doing his job.

By now he had a full grown beard and a hint of his beloved ponytail. On one of the few days off, he went home to his folk's house. His mother was in decline. It hurt to watch, knowing he could do nothing about it. Martin was home from Seminary and they were comparing the length of their hair. His father was just shaking his head, "The world gone totally upside down. My sons have ponytails and my daughter has a crew cut."

Indeed Joanna had discovered goth culture. She was just a freshman in high school and had shaved her head awhile back. She found herself grounded for a month and still was kept on a tight leash by Mark. Mary had found it rather amusing and softened the blow somewhat. It was just growing back. Michael studied her features. She was so beautiful. He never could understand why life was so hard for her. He saw girls like her on a daily basis at the bar and with the gang members. Why were they there? What had happened in their lives to bring them to where they were? The family knew of course, that he was a police officer undercover, but that was all they knew. If they needed him for some reason they had to go through his boss, Detective Morris, and explain why. It seemed a cumbersome process and had the effect of keeping Michael out of touch with the family. He understood why things had to be this way but, particularly at moments like this, with them all together again watching their mother die, it ripped at his soul. At this point he was deep enough in that his discovery could lead to retaliation on his family. He had already seen retaliation and it was worse than ugly. Inflict the most physical and emotional damage as you could. He couldn't imagine how he could ever explain to Martin how he had encouraged a group one night to 'just' gang rape a 14 year old rather than cut her to ribbons and leave her to die or be scared for the rest of her life. He also couldn't see explaining that to his handlers. Those were the kind of things that Alex, his undercover name, had to do to survive, to get deeper, to cut off the head of the snake. He told himself he was getting close.

It was three more years before he became a lieutenant in the gang. He had been involved in a shooting when an upstart group jumped him and Mitch. Michael had killed one of the rivals and wounded another. It cemented him with Mitch, the head of the gang but raised some concerns with his handler. He had to fill out a lot of paperwork. It was ultimately put down as self defense and buried in a file somewhere. That was a year before this visit home and by now he had most of the information they wanted; the head of the organization, the name and location of the supply chain and access to the book of payments to the cops, judges and petty politicians who were on the payroll.

They had almost everything they wanted except taped conversations confirming enough information to give credence to the indictment. They had some tapes of phone conversations but the warrants for them were subject to question. Getting them accepted would be open to challenge. There were to be no holes in this case. Mike had to wear a wire for a bit. This was a problem in Mike's mind. He had made friends in the gang. He had a girlfriend who had been an active participant in some pretty ugly stuff. He had to find a way to get wired up and avoid any intimate contact with Kate till he could get the damned thing off; before any hugs or intimacy.

Kate and a lot of the other girls were just pawns; basically, just taking part in the only way of life they had ever known. It was the best of the few choices they had. They were just like many of his classmates in the academy, going along with what they were told. They were as much victims as those the gang took advantage of.

There was no choice of course and Mike, or Alex as it were, was taped with a wireless mic to his chest and went to a council meeting. He got everything they wanted and more when a city councilman's name came up. There was to be a planned hit; a verifiable action on tape that chimed the bell. A rival councilman was causing problems and needed to be taken out. Time to bring this to an end. The hit man was an outsider called only Angel. He had already been paid an advance of $20,000. Apparently, nobody had actually met this guy or knew who he was except by reputation. He was a professional. It got heated about how they could trust a phantom. That proved to be the best part of the meeting as far as the D.A. was concerned. The arguing factions were calling each other by name and bringing up previous hits. It was everything they could have hoped for and Mike got the credit. The biggest bonus was that now they didn't need Mike's testimony. He would not need to be exposed. They never found out the identity of the hit man but with the gang wrapped up, there was no way to receive the balance due on the contract and they eventually let it drop. They staged a shooting during the initial bust and made it appear that Mike was killed.

Thirty-four convictions in all, including eighteen police officers. Mike lived his life as a bartender for another year in a distant corner of the city until the trial was over. He was quietly moved into a station on the other side of the city and promoted to Detective. A year later he broke the murder of Officer Palmer. It was impossible to keep him out of the press, but if anyone made the connection, they kept it to themselves. A handful of his fellow officers, mostly classmates, knew who he was though, and figured that's why he'd moved so fast within the department. That was also the first time he met the widow Palmer and her young daughter.

Chapter 9

Friday, May 4, 2018

Friday morning Michael and Jennifer arrived at the school with a whole new set of questions. Jennifer had spoken with Maggie's parents and cleared the way to conduct the interview at the school. Once it was clear that Maggie was just being asked for background they had deferred attending, leaving the responsibility to Mrs. Hartner, the principal. She had Maggie Sanford called to the office.

While waiting for Maggie to arrive, Mrs. Hartner asked, "you understand we will have a counselor present detective? She's a minor and we serve as 'in loco parentis'."

"Of course," Jennifer replied. "We just need to get some background on Marissa. By the way, thank you for your quick response on the request for her records. They arrived at the station this morning."

"We also are interested in the girl who was with her when she went to check on Marissa" added Michael.

"Terrible times we're living in," said Mrs. Hartner.

The door to the office opened and a male about thirty-two entered.

"This is our guidance counselor, Arthur Bennet. Art, these are detectives Davis and Palmer. As you know, they have some questions for Maggie."

"Pleased to meet you detectives." Art shook their extended hands.

Mike didn't find anything unusual, but Jennifer took an instant dislike to this man. Just a gut response. She had learned to put those feelings in the back of her mind, but not very far back.

The door opened again and Maggie Sanford sheepishly entered the room.

"Hi Maggie. I'm Detective Palmer. Detective Davis and I just want to ask you a little about your friend Marissa if that's ok. You can call me Jen if you prefer."

"Well Detective I don't know that I can help much."

"You've already helped a great deal, Maggie. If you hadn't tried to find out what was wrong, this whole thing could have been much more complicated. Would you mind telling us who the girl was that was with you at the apartment house? Do you think it would be possible for her to join us?"

Maggie loved the idea of having a friend present but, before she could respond, the principal interrupted. "I'm not sure I can allow that. I know that you've cleared this with Mr. and Mrs. Sanford. I'd have to get the consent of the parents of anyone additional."

"Of course," Michael stepped in. "That would not be a problem. I'm sure the other young lady has probably already told her parents about the experience. Why don't we check? Who was with you Maggie?"

"Nancy Drew," answered Maggie.

Art saw the look on the detective's faces. "That's really her name," he said. "Apparently, her parents thought it would be cute," Art said with a shrug of his shoulders. The hairs on the back of Jen's neck started to rise slightly. He was a little too nonchalant for her liking.

It took about 20 minutes to get Nancy and her parent's agreement. They had tried to pass the time with small talk but it was becoming more and more uncomfortable. Everyone seemed quite relieved when Nancy came in the room. The room designed for four people was now up to six. Another chair was pulled in for Nancy. Maggie seemed far more comfortable now that her friend was beside her. It had been decided that Jennifer would lead the questioning. Michael stood with his back to the door and Mr. Bennet sat with one cheek resting on the credenza behind Mrs. Hartner's desk.

"I want to thank you ladies for your help in this terrible thing. I'm sure you're both still in shock." Jennifer avoided the word murder. "We understand that both of you have been friends of Marissa's for a number of years and we were hoping that you could tell us a little about her; where she hung out, boyfriends, anything you can think of that might help."

The girls looked at each other nervously and glanced at Mr. Bennet before they answered. "Well," Maggie started, "I guess you know about the problem she had last year?"

"Yes" Jennifer replied. "We've spoken to Mr. Collins already. Unfortunate. It must have been very hard for her."

"Oh, you can't imagine. Really tore her up mentally. She changed a lot after that." Nancy jumped in. Mike saw the nudge Maggie gave her as she spoke.

"Well she did," Nancy said, turning to Maggie.

"If you girls would be more comfortable doing this downtown with your parents present we...," Michael started to say, remembering how well it had worked on Mr. Collins, but Maggie interrupted.

"No. This is fine. She was a good friend. We just don't want to give you the wrong impression."

"And how would you do that?" asked Jennifer.

"Well, she had a lot of friends after that. You know, boys, and a few men."

"I see," said Jennifer. "I understand you want to protect your friend's reputation but we're trying to catch her killer."

Jennifer gave that a minute to sink in. "Was there anybody that was threatening her that you know of?"

"Well." Again a glance at Mr. Bennet. Was it Jen's imagination? Her dislike of this man had raised her attention, or was it just a teenager's resistance to rat out her friend? "There was no one I can think of who would actually want her dead," Maggie said. Nancy shrugged her shoulders in agreement.

"I wonder if you know the names of the two boys who got into an argument at her apartment about a month ago."

"Oh that. That was just Judd and Larry. Judd got arrested, but they are just like that. Larry was always trying to protect Mar. He was her self-appointed protector. He's been a friend since grade school. She never paid him much attention, but he was always hanging around. Marissa called him when Judd wouldn't quit banging on her door. Judd never got in the apartment and Larry took a pretty good beating by the time the cops got there. Judd's a hot head and a bully but he'd never kill anybody. He had to go to court. I'm sure you could find the info on that. The case was dismissed. Larry wouldn't press charges."

"Would it be possible for you to tell us why Marissa was so, eh, popular?"

"Well," they looked at each other searching for what to say. "She was very pretty."

"Both of you are quite attractive. Are you as popular?" Jen asked.

"What they are trying not to say," Mr. Bennet interjected, "is that Marissa was promiscuous."

Mrs. Hartner, the principal, spoke up. "I'm not sure that's appropriate Art"

"Who are we kidding, Betty? We all know what was going on."

The two girls looked startled that Marissa life was being dissected right in front of them.

"Is that true, ladies?" asked Jennifer. They hesitated long enough for Jennifer to add, "a large amount of cash and expensive items were found in Marissa's bedroom."

"That didn't have anything to do with the boys," Nancy volunteered. "That was from her men friends."

"She just kind of used them for gifts," Maggie joined in.

"Did you happen to know any of these men?" asked Jennifer. She glanced over at Mr. Bennet, who looked noticeably disturbed by the turn the questioning had taken.

"Now this may be approaching some inappropriate areas," he interjected.

"Just a few more questions, Mr. Bennet," Jennifer said, and while looking straight at him asked the girls, "do either of you know who happened to be the father of Marissa's unborn baby?"

"Hell no!" Nancy said.

"Maggie?"

"Well, I'd prefer not to say ma'am."

"I understand your reluctance. Let me ask in a different way. Do either of you know where the abortion was conducted?" Jennifer pursued.

"I believe it was at Magee Women's in Oakland. Why?" Maggie asked.

"They would maintain blood samples and DNA that would identify the father," she replied still, looking at Mr. Bennet.

The blood was visibly draining from Art Bennet's face. Part of the problem solved, thought Jennifer. She returned her focus to the girls. "I certainly hope neither of you is mixed up further in any of this."

Both girls were on the verge of tears. It was quite obvious to anyone in the room what had just happened. "No ma'am. We were just trying to be friends."

"Do you happen to know the names of any of her men friends?" Jennifer asked.

"No, ma'am. Honest," Nancy answered. Maggie just shook her head.

"Well, we will be pursuing this for some time. We may have some more questions later, but if you think of anything else that might help, I can be reached at this number." She handed them each a business card. "We really appreciate your help. You've been very good friends to Marissa. Unless Detective Davis has anything else, I think you can return to class."

"No. I'm good," said Michael, astonished by what he'd just witnessed. A mother's instinct he thought. He was having a hard time not smiling.

"If you ladies need some time to gather yourselves, you may go to the nurse's office. If you want to call your folks I'll give you a note to use the phone" Mrs. Hartner said. Both girls pulled out their cell phones to indicate they would not need the phone. "I think we'll just go to the nurse's office for a minute or two" said Maggie.

After the girls had left, Michael said to Mr. Arthur Bennet, "I think you might want to come downtown with us. We have a few more questions for you."

"I didn't kill her," Art blurted out. "I may have crossed a line, but I didn't kill her."

"You best come with us," said Jennifer. "Currently you're under arrest for suspicion of statutory rape. You have the right to remain silent. If you choose to not remain silent anything you say can and will be used.....

Their voices drifted away as Mrs. Hartner stood, mouth agape, in the doorway of her office.

Chapter 10

6 years ago.

Jennifer Palmer was at home in her kitchen when she heard the knock on the door. She was comfortably dressed in jeans and a polo shirt. She still had an apron on as was her custom when baking. Funny she thought, I don't wear an apron for cooking dinner, only when I'm baking. Guess it's because of the flour. There's something about flour that just screams for an apron. She wiped her hands on the apron as she crossed the living room and answered the door. Her knees buckled when she saw Deputy Chief Templeton and another officer standing in front of her. No cop's wife needed to ask why they were there. Injuries, they send a car to take you to the hospital. Overtime, they call. But only one thing brings the Deputy Chief.

Templeton caught her by the waist and eased her into the first chair he came to in the living room.

"He's alive, Mrs. Palmer," Templeton said quickly to steady Jennifer. "But it's not good. He was shot in the head and is in surgery. I'm here to accompany you to the hospital."

"Of course. Let me just turn off the stove," Jennifer replied mechanically. "Oh! What about Meagan?"

"I brought an officer who can stay with her."

A female officer that Jennifer sort of recognized as a friend of Jim's appeared in the doorway. "Don't worry Jennifer; I'll take care of the stove. I can finish whatever you were working on. Where is Meagan now?"

"She's playing next door. She'll be home any minute."

As she was answering, Bonnie Able, her-next door neighbor appeared next to Jennifer. She was quite a bit older than Jennifer, but had a daughter, Emily, about the same age as

Meagan. The two kids had grown up together and considered both households as one. "Is everything ok? I saw the police cars..." Bonnie stopped mid-sentence when she saw Jennifer. "I've got this," she said. "She'll stay and have dinner with us. She can stay over if necessary. The kids are out back. They haven't noticed anything yet. Jen? Jen, are you ok?"

Amid the confusion around her, Jennifer had started to regain her composure. "I'm not sure yet Bonnie, but thanks. That will help a lot. I need to go to the hospital. If you haven't started dinner yet, you can take what's in the kitchen. Just lock up when you leave. You're a dear." She looked at the female officer. "It's Barbara, isn't it?" she asked. Barbara nodded. "Thank you very much, but Meagan will be fine with Bonnie. Let me get my purse."

There wasn't much conversation on the way to the hospital; just a few details. It was a traffic stop. No one knew any details yet. A car matching the description of a stolen vehicle. Somehow the driver got the drop on Jim. The perpetrator was still at large. Other than that, just silence on the drive to the hospital. When they arrived, Jen understood why Deputy Chief Templeton had come. The doctor who met them explained that Jim was just out of surgery and it would be a while till they would know much. He was in a coma. If he lived, he would probably be a paraplegic. The blood was draining from Jennifer's face again, but she maintained both her balance and her composure. "Can I see him?" Jen asked. "Of course, Mrs. Palmer," the doctor replied. "But you need to know it's pretty bad. At least one of the bullets was to the face. He's heavily bandaged."

Jennifer entered the area in CCU, closed off by curtains. She dropped into a chair near the bed, dropped her head into her hands, and cried.

An officer named Peterson or Paterson or something like that, she wasn't really sure, dropped her off at her home a few hours later.

"Would you like me to go in with you, Mrs. Palmer?" he asked.

"No officer. I'll be ok. But thanks for offering."

Jennifer unlocked the front door and did two things. First, she called Bonnie. "Is she ok? Great. It'll be easier to explain to her in the morning. No. Thanks but I'm fine. Yes, it's bad, real bad. Give me a headsup before she comes back in the morning, Bonnie. I can't thank you enough." Then she went into the den and took a letter out of the right-hand drawer of the desk. It was addressed to Jim, telling him that she was leaving him. She walked into the living room, took a strike-anywhere match from the box on the hearth, lit one end of the envelope, held it until she was sure it caught and tossed it into the fireplace.

It took almost 6 months for Jim to die. He never left the hospital and never regained consciousness. Jennifer had fallen into a routine and Meagan, after a short period of adjustment, returned to being a six year old. Between the little bit they had saved, the mortgage insurance, and Jim's pension and insurance from the department, she and Meagan were fairly secure; at least for the immediate future. She discovered that being alone wasn't much different than the last few years of her marriage.

Chapter 11

Saturday, May 5, 2018

Saturday morning found Michael and Jennifer back at their desks in the squad room of Precinct 1. Their desks were back to back. It amused Mike that the room looked like the set of a TV show. Reality models fiction. It all looked so easy on TV, he thought.

"What are you smiling about?" Jennifer asked.

The squad room was typical Saturday slow. Some clean up from the usual Friday night mix-ups that escalated enough to rise to the Detective level; a domestic that lead to a death; nothing to equal the mystery that they were working on.

"Oh nothing. Just daydreaming. What do you have Meagan up to today?," Michael replied.

"She's going skating with some friends. I was hoping to be home around 3 so we could have a normal family dinner. Maybe take in a movie tonight."

"Let's just compare notes and plan for Monday then," Michael said, knowing that his few notes would be worthless compared to Jennifer's.

Jennifer looked at the single sheet of paper on top of the file she had put together and left for Michael. "Well, we have the sister to interview. We need to see if we can find out where Marissa and Lily Carpenter were in the twenty- four hours prior to the murders. We need to talk to these Judd and Larry characters, speaking of which, I want to follow up on our friend Mr. Arthur Bennet. I want to see the book thrown at him. I already checked, there were no other police calls to the household or apartment building for that matter in the last six months. I have the boys, last names and addresses from the report on the disturbance; appears to be a rather innocuous fistfight between the boys. Neither pressed charges. It's just an incident report."

Michael, who had a single scrap of paper smoothed out on his desk, replied, "Well we've nothing new from the autopsies or ballistics. DNA has not come back from the lab, so I guess we prioritize your list and call it a day."

Jennifer looked at him as he balled up the scrap of paper and tossed it into the wire trash can beside his desk. "Guess you're not much of a note-taker. Must have been a barrel of laughs in college."

"Good memory, quick study. I did ok," Michael replied, adding "So what do you have on tap for tomorrow?"

"Not sure yet. Have to talk to that little creature I chauffer around in my spare time. Why? I hope you're not planning on working tomorrow. It's been a pretty intense week."

"No, no work. It's just that I happen to have a couple extra tickets to 'Swan Lake' at the Benedum tomorrow night. As you said, it's been a long week and I thought maybe you and Meag might like to join me. I realize it's short notice but these just fell into my lap."

"Oh Michael, I don't know. Meagan would love it, but." She hesitated, "protocol and all. It kind of looks like a date."

"Screw that. It's for Meagan. If you're really concerned, here you can take the tickets and I'll stay home," he said. "I'm sure that someone is playing football Sunday on TV."

"Oh Michael, don't get that way. You know how it would look. You're not the most popular guy around here. I don't want to get you in any trouble."

"I'm well aware of where I stand around here; young-hot shot, loner. Who knows what he really did while undercover all those years? I've heard it; I'm aware but you know what? Fuck 'em. They didn't live it; they don't know what it does to you. Make friends just to betray them. See how other people live, what they do to stay alive. They all think it's a trick, a holiday from regulations, a chance to have some fun. I'll tell you Jen, it's not at all fun. It rips at your insides. It eats at your soul. I solve cases because I understand what it's like to walk in those shoes; to run, even if it means a shot in the back rather than give up the miserable existence you scratched out of the only life you've ever known."

Jennifer could see his face reddening, his eyes dilating. "Michael, it's ok. You don't need to do this. I know who you really are. I don't need an explanation." She paused for a moment and then continued "Let's do it! Tomorrow night; you, me and Meagan. But separate cars. No reason to push it. And it's just the ballet, ok?"

"Yeah, sounds great," said Michael brightening up instantly. "And I'm sorry. You don't need that shit."

"Promise to watch your language around Meagan."

"Of course. Sorry again."

Chapter 12

Saturday, May 5, 2018; 9:45pm

    St. Paul's Roman Catholic Church was the antithesis of St. Anne's. It was only a few towns further south on Route 65 but it didn't have the stable population that St. Anne's enjoyed and it didn't have a mysterious benefactor. It had never had a convent or a school attached, and while the architecture was well done Gothic, it had suffered the wear of time and lack of funds. The carefully cut stones were a remnant of the Pittsburgh that earned it's name of the smoky city. Their careful cuts and the once gray mortar blackened by time and neglect. The elder of the two prefects there was Father Costello, well into his eighties and very fixed in his ways. He had always objected to the changes in the church. He loved the Latin mass and had no interest in turning the altar to face the people. The mysticism had gone out of him along with the church. He always took the late Saturday confessional duties. The few youth left in the church had learned to go to confession on Friday or early Saturday rather than face the lectures of old Father Costello. His penances were always long and tedious; his criticisms longer. And so Father William James Costello sat in his alb and penitent stole waiting for sinners in need of forgiveness. He carefully weighed the required penance necessary for atonement. God's graces required sincerity he reminded them.

    The church was empty. The confessional booth had its dim light lit indicating both sides were vacant, waiting for the penitent to enter. A sole figure walked down the center aisle and eased its way through the pews to the left chamber of the confessional, pulled the curtain aside, and went in and knelt. The sound of the wooden window cover reverberated through the church as Father Costello prepared to hear the sins of the confessor.

    "Bless me Father for I have sinned. It has been longer than I can remember since my last confession. I have committed an act

I am having difficulty living with. It is a mortal sin that rests uneasy on my soul."

"My son, God forgives all truly repentant souls, but that is a great time between confessions. Why have you been absent from the sacrament so long?"

"There are things, Father, that happen outside the church; things so removed from the sacraments yet necessary in everyday life, things I do not wish to argue now. It is this one sin, Father that keeps me awake at night; that I know was wrong. I must have that forgiven. I must."

"What could this sin be that has you so distraught my child?" Father Costello asked.

"I murdered an innocent soul."

Momentary silence from the center of the confessional until finally Father Costello whispered "This is a grave sin, my son. What could have led to you committing this action?"

"She could identify me Father. I couldn't take that chance."

"Identify you? I don't understand." Father Costello was searching his mind for the right thing to say. His head was swimming in dark waters; murder? Identity? What was he to do? He reached deep for clarity. Was this to be my test Lord? he thought.

"Well Father, circumstances had made it necessary for me to remove a sinner. It is something I do for a living although this one was not an assignment. She was just a temptation to distract me from my work. The woman I murdered would have been an innocent bystander. I did not have to kill her but she could identify me."

By now Father Costello was in panic. What was happening he thought? "My son" he blurted out. "What are you saying? You killed two people?"

The panic in his voice gave him away. "They call me Angel," the voice from the confessional said as he silently screwed the silencer onto the barrel of his pistol. "I remove sinners from their paths. But this one was not a sinner in that way. She did not have to die. Can God forgive me father? What is my penance?"

The 9mm pistol hung by his side, gripped in his right hand while in his mind he kept saying, "forgive me father, forgive me father. Please forgive me. Give me my penance."

"God forgives all the truly repentant, my son." Father Costello's voice was quivering as he spoke. "For your penance you must go forth and commit to sin no more. You must make a sincere act of contrition and turn yourself in to the authorities. This cannot..."

A small sound, similar to opening a can of soda, reported from the confessional. Angel stepped out from behind the left curtain, looked around and, seeing no one present, opened the center door. Father Costello was hunched over in his wooden chair, the purple pall around his neck stained with the blood running down from his right temple. Angel fired one more shot through the center of his dropped head and whispered to himself, "You should have given me absolution." The lifeless body fell to the floor in front of Angel. He noticed that his eyes were still open. He carefully used the pall to close the eyes. He turned, collected the spent cartridges and shuffled back through the closest row of pews. Upon entering the center aisle, he turned and genuflected to the altar, made the sign of the cross and, turning again, put a fifty dollar bill in the poor box and walked quietly out of the church.

Chapter 13

Michael's preparations for the theater were interrupted by the phone. He had spent his morning listening to some smooth jazz, the afternoon was spent in his shop setting the templates he made for the kitchen island he was building and he felt pleased with what he'd accomplished. Although he tried not to, he had frequently found his thoughts leaning toward Jennifer. He'd just stepped out of the shower when the phone rang. The first thought he had was that it was Jennifer with some reason why they could not go to the ballet tonight. His heart sunk in his chest. He felt relief at the sound of Deputy Chief Detective Bob Morrow's voice on the line.

"There was another shooting last night. Father Costello was shot assassination-style in the confessional at St. Paul's; in the fucking confessional for Christ's sake. Is no place safe anymore?"

"That's outside our jurisdiction Bob. Why are you calling me?"

"The initial ballistics indicates a 9mm. No shells casings, no prints. Sound familiar?"

"Bob, I worked six days last week; all at least 9 hours. Can't I have at least one day to myself? Jennifer and I can look into it tomorrow. Have they reached out for help? The locals can be pretty territorial."

"Better. The Bishop called and asked that we look into it. He specifically asked for you. Clear sailing Mike."

"Bob, that's great, but I've got plans for the evening. It'll have to wait till tomorrow and if it doesn't connect to our current case, we'll have to hand it off. We still have too many loose ends on the Carpenter case."

"Ok Mike. The file will be on your desk in the morning, but my gut tells me it's the same guy."

Mike set his phone to airplane mode. No more calls for at least an hour he thought. He was standing in his bedroom, in his boxer shorts, staring into his closet. This is ridiculous, he thought. "It's not a date, it's not a date. She's just my partner; this is for Meagan. Just pick a suit. It's no biggie."

In his past life Michael, or rather Alex, had lived the life of a banger. Sex for the hell of it flowed with the coke and booze. More than once he had awakened in a strange bed or in his own with some girl he didn't know. He had eventually hooked up with Kate during his last three years undercover. In many ways that was even worse. How do you get over lying to a lover? She thinks he's dead. It was the easiest way to get him out. It's been hell getting her out of his head, not because he loved her, but because he hurt her. He lived in dread of running into her on the street, or worse, on a case. And in moments, alone in his apartment or is his bed, he missed her in other ways. The soft warmth of her form pressing against him; the subtle motions, gradually raising in intensity, increasing in pitch and tone, faster, harder, building, holding, clutching, ripping, tearing and, and, and...end. Yes, there were other things he missed but he couldn't afford to think of any of that at the moment. He knew that he was drawn to Jennifer and had to walk a fine line; at least for a while.

Michael wound up with a simple navy blue suit, white shirt, school stripe tie, waiting in the lobby of the Benedum with three tickets in hand. The tickets had been a gift from an old high school friend who was now on the editorial staff of The Pittsburgh Post Gazette. Michael had managed to extricate his son from some trouble with a minor marijuana buy earlier in the year. He hadn't even looked at the seats until now: first balcony right, first row: very nice.

The morning and afternoon were a little different for Jennifer.

"You won't let me go see Katy Perry, but its ok for you to drag me to some ballet."

"Meagan, I told you that you could go to see Katy Perry. You just need to be accompanied by a parent or adult. You're not ready to be left alone in that massive stadium. I'm sorry. Anyway, it was Michael's idea. He got the ticket from a friend and remembered you took ballet so..."

"That was eons ago. I was only ten," and immediately brightened and added, "Michael remembered that I took ballet?"

"Well now you're only thirteen. You don't want to hurt his feelings do you?"

"Oh, I like Michael but I have a feeling it was more you he wanted to take and I'll be just tagging along."

"Don't be silly, we're just partners. That's all."

"Yeah, right. Now who's the teenager Mom?"

"Even if you were right, it would be none of your business young lady. Right now, we have to find you a dress."

"I still don't see why I can't just throw on a skirt and blouse."

"It's a grand opening Meag. This is a big deal. There will be people in tuxedos and gowns. The mayor will probably be there. I wouldn't be surprised to see some celebrities. We have to go buy you a new dress, a slip, new bra, panty hose without a tear in them"...

The idea of a new bra lit up Meagan's mind. Yeah, she was a woman now. They should go to Victoria's Secret. And maybe thigh highs instead of panty hose. Jennifer saw the transformation instantly and realized it was going to be one of those shopping trips. Why can't kids just wait to grow up?, she thought.

Three hours later, worn to the quick from rationalizing, bickering, cajoling, and outright fighting, they walked through the doors of the Benedum. Jennifer was wearing a very tasteful-off-the-shoulder navy blue evening dress, a couple inches above the knee, with matching heels. Meagan had on a new spaghetti-strap, floral print dress, somewhat shorter than her mother's and a new pair of two-inch high heels from Nordstroms. But what she was proudest of was her new strapless bra. She had won that battle. She had also won the battle on using the valet parking. "Mother, I can't walk a couple blocks in these new heels. They'll get all scuffed up." After they entered the foyer, Jennifer stopped and looked at her little girl. It gave her a mixed feeling of pride and loss at the same time.

Michael spotted them. He was as unaccustomed to playing dress up as Meagan and was taken aback by how absolutely beautiful Jennifer looked. He realized that this was the first time he'd seen her with makeup, dressed to the nines. He instantly thought that he should have rented a tux. And Meagan! Could this really be her? No blue jeans and sneakers. This was not the little tomboy he knew. He also was lost somewhere between pride that these two women were with him and the sensation of being a misfit. He was not at all sure he could pull this off. He snapped out of it, driven by the force of the crowd, and made his way over to them. Everything in him wanted to lean over and give Jennifer a kiss but he knew better. Keep it cool he told himself. He reached out and took Meagan's hand and bowing, kissed the back of it. Looking straight at Meagan he said to Jennifer, "And who is this fine lady, Ms. Palmer?"

"Oh Michael, you're so silly," Meagan replied.

Jennifer took his other hand and gave it a squeeze. He thought to himself "everything's going to be just fine." He smiled at Jennifer and led them over to an usher to help find their seats. He knew they were good seats, but didn't have any idea how they would get there.

"Let's get seated first and then if you want refreshments we can come back down." While he'd been waiting, he'd discovered that there was a lounge below the entry level that offered canapés, a cash bar and restrooms. After all, he didn't want to look like he'd never been here before, even though he hadn't. He followed the overhead signs to the balcony and found it was a hallway along the right side of the foyer. There was an usher at the entrance. The usher looked at the tickets and led them up a flight of stairs and down a long corridor, passing doors on their left. It seemed a far distance. They came to the last door on the left and the usher led them through, walked to the first row and brushed the seats off with a white cloth that seemed to appear out of nowhere, and extended his hand motioning for them to sit. Michael looked at the usher and realized that he was really just some college kid and that he was supposed to tip him. This shook him back to reality and he fished a five out of his pocket and handed it to him. The kid looked disappointed. After all, these were five hundred dollar seats, each; only a crummy five? Michael picked up on it and reached back into his pocket and came back with an additional ten. The kid looked at him and grinned, shrugged his shoulders and departed.

Michael then looked at Jennifer and Meagan. Their eyes were as wide as could be. Below them was the entire stage and in front of that the orchestra pit. The floor was a buzz of people. The musicians were all tuning up their instruments. The cacophony of sounds was unbelievable. After staring over the rail in front of them in amazement for a while they settled back into their seats. Jennifer was in seat 1, Meagan was between them in 2 and Michael was next to her. There was an empty seat on the aisle.

"Would either of you care to go down to the lounge? We have a few minutes before the performance begins?" Michael asked. About then the lights dimmed and came back up immediately. "I think that means we have about ten minutes," Michael said.

Jennifer looked at Meagan. "Ladies room?," she asked.

"No, I'm fine," Meagan answered. "Oh, did you want to sit next to Michael?" she asked.

Jennifer gave her an elbow in the ribs while replying with a forced smile," No, this is fine"

Michael caught it immediately and shot a quick grin to Jennifer.

About then two couples were led into the balcony. Michael was trying to quietly see what they tipped the usher. He noticed that it was a fifty. A voice behind him asked, "Mike? Aren't you Mike Davis?"

Michael stood up and turned around and found himself looking right into the face of the Mayor himself. Jennifer turned and, when she recognized the Mayor, stood herself.

"Why yes, Mr. Mayor, and this is my partner, Jennifer Palmer, and her daughter Meagan."

"This is my wife, Diana, and I believe you know my Deputy Chief of staff, Mr. Cousins and his wife Emily. I was just talking to Bob Morrow about you earlier."

"Yes sir. He called me. Detective Palmer and I will be taking that up first thing tomorrow. I haven't even had time to brief her yet."

"Well I can certainly understand why. No reason to deal with that on such a pleasant evening. Palmer...Palmer. Were you the wife of"

Jennifer's eye's flared, first at the Mayor and then toward her daughter. The Mayor caught on immediately. "No. That was something else I was thinking about." He looked down at Meagan, who was staring back at him and said with a grin, "Mayors get easily confused." Looking back at Jennifer he said, "Terrible business you're working on now though. Just terrible."

Meagan looked at her mother and just rolled her eyes. "Well mom, you said we might see the Mayor here tonight." She looked over at Michael who could see she was trying hard not to laugh.

The lights dimmed again only this time for a little longer. Everyone took their seats. Meagan stood up and, turning around, put her hand out to the Mayor, "It's a pleasure to meet you sir." This time it was Jennifer who rolled her eyes.

The orchestra started, the curtain went up and the dancers took the stage. As much as she tried to be a detached teenager, Meagan was in wonderland, totally captivated by the performance. It turned out that she was actually the only one in the entire group who knew the story the ballet told and the progression of movements the dances represented. She wound up explaining to the six adults what was going on. It greatly helped to relieve the tension that they had been feeling individually and made these very disparate souls find common ground for the evening.

At intermission they all went down to the lounge together and the Mayor was introducing Meagan to all of these people while she explained the background of the story. She was in her glory but secretly wondered why all these people were at a show they knew nothing about. He also insisted on buying both Michael and Jennifer a glass of wine. When they were able to get a moment alone, Michael said to Jennifer, "I hope this doesn't come back to bite us in the ass." Jennifer wanted to know what was going on with this case they were taking up the next morning. Michael filled her in briefly. As the lights dimmed the first time, Meagan grabbed Jennifer's hand and said, "Why don't we go freshen up Mother?" Jennifer just rolled her eyes and followed her daughter.

The second movement went much like the first with Meagan spending most of her time explaining to the Mayor, who she was now calling Bill, how the dancer's movements reflected their emotions and what was happening in the story. Jennifer was absolutely astounded at her daughter's breadth of knowledge about the ballet. She didn't have a clue that Meagan knew all this, and wondered how Michael had known how much it would mean to Meagan.

At the conclusion of the ballet, after three curtain calls, both parties rose to leave. The Mayor put his hand on Michael's shoulder and said, "I had no idea you had such refined taste in both art and women, especially you young lady." And looking right at Meagan, "I'll see what I can do about that other thing we talked about." After they had all shook hands and entered the line exiting the theater, Jennifer put her hand on her daughter's arm and said to her, "What was that all about and how did you become an expert on Swan Lake?"

"Oh, just something I mentioned to Bill in the lounge. Not important mother."

Michael turned to look at Meagan. "You made all that up, didn't you?"

Meagan broke into a big grin. "You are a good detective Michael." Michael slipped her a high five. Jennifer's face started to drain of all color.

"Don't worry about it, Jen. It was close enough. He'll never know the difference."

When they finally got to the foyer Michael offered to walk them to their car. Jennifer just held up the valet ticket and looked directly at Meagan and said, "Another reason I'm glad we took separate cars." Meagan still had a big grin on her face and she thought, "I'm going to get a lecture, but it was worth it."

"I'll see you in the morning, Michael." The tone of her voice let him know that he was in for a lecture also.

Chapter 14

Monday May 7, 2018

Jennifer stopped dead in the doorway of the squad room. Their desks had been pushed up into the aisle leaving only a small path to walk. In the space that had opened up was an old-fashioned blackboard; the type on wheels with a wooden frame and a surface that could be flipped over. On the side she could see there was a number 6 in chalk with a circle around it. From left to right, after the number, was a picture of Marissa and next to that, about a foot away, was a picture of Lily. Below the number 6 was a column headed 'interviewed' with a list of the people they had already talked to: Ted Collins, ex; Jim Blocker, super; Maggie Sanford, friend; Nancy Drew, friend. Adjacent to that was a second heading, 'To Interview'. Below this one was: April Carpenter, sister; Judd Roman, boyfriend?; Larry Roberts, protector? Under Marissa's photo was written 'Where Abouts?' and below that 'Phone' underlined. Under Lily's picture was 'Where Abouts?'; 'Partner?'

"What's with the blackboard?" Jennifer asked.

"Helps me think," Michael answered.

"You know I have all that on an excel spreadsheet," she replied.

"Not the same" he said. "Just something I do sometimes. I think it has something to do with the physical act of writing. It internalizes it somehow."

"And the 6?" she asked.

"Days we've been on the case. The longer it goes the tougher it gets. Leads go cold." Michael said.

"Well, what's next?" Jennifer asked.

Michael flipped the board over. On the top right was the number 1 with a circle around it and next to it a picture of Father Costello, this time with his name underneath the photo. There was nothing else on the board. "This is what the Mayor was referring to last night. It's been added to our case load, courtesy of the Bishop and the Mayor.

"Why? It's not even in our jurisdiction?" said Jennifer.

"The Deputy Chief thinks they may be connected. Professional job, weapon appears to be a 9mm, maybe with a silencer."

"Now what?"

"Well, I guess we start with a run out to St. Paul's. Check out the crime scene. You can call Lily's sister on the way. See if she can see us around one. Gives us two to three hours to talk to anyone at the church. Oh, did you find out what Meagan's deal was with the Mayor?"

"Not a word. She was like a stone."

"And here I thought you were a good interviewer" Michael shot back with a grin. Jennifer gave him an elbow in the ribs, picked up her purse and her laptop and headed for the car.

The crime scene inside the left side of the nave was still marked off with yellow 'police line' tape, but the church was empty except for a lone figure kneeling at the foot of the altar. Michael recognized the ponytailed figure immediately.

"Marty, surprised to see you here." His younger brother was a couple inches taller than Michael but much slimmer. Father Martin Davis stood and turned around. The resemblance was unmistakable; same thick shock of chestnut hair, strong jaw, very light complexion, unmistakably Irish ancestry.

"Ah, Mickey! How did this mess wind up in your lap?" Father Martin said. "And is this your new partner?"

"Detective Jennifer Palmer, meet my baby brother, Father Martin Davis. Assistant Pastor and Youth Minister at Saint Ann's in Ambridge. As far as the case, the Bishop specifically requested I work the case with the locals. You didn't have anything to do with that, did you?"

"Good heavens no, although I must admit that it's good to see you in a church. I promised dad I'd bring you and Joanna back to the flock before you die."

"Is that our father or The Father, Marty?"

"Both,Michael; it wouldn't kill you to worry about your soul. "

"Yeah, we already had that conversation a few times. Now is not the best time to revisit my soul," Michael replied. "So what are you doing here?"

"Helping to fill in till they can find a priest to assign. We're a vanishing breed, if you haven't heard. I think it has to do with that celibacy thing. The recent press on the behavior of a few deviants hasn't helped much either; weakness of the flesh, and the hierarchy didn't help much by their handling of the problem," Martin said shaking his head. "Would I be out of line asking if you happen to be a Catholic, Ms. Palmer?"

"Close but not quite; Episcopalian Father" answered Jennifer.

"Close enough," said Martin. "Call me Martin, it's much more comfortable."

"By any chance do you have any clues about who would do this, Martin?" Michael asked. "Anybody excommunicated recently? Any rumors about Father Costello's behavior that might invite retaliation? Maybe an exorcism?," asked Michael.

"Nothing that I know of, Michael. I would tell you if there was, but I'll keep my ear to the ground. In the damned confessional! I can't quite shake it. Raises the hairs on the back of my neck."

"That would be a big wave," said Michael, yanking his brother's ponytail.

"Easy brother. It wasn't that long ago that you cut yours off," Martin replied.

"He was found by Father John Andres. Do you know much about him?" Jennifer asked.

"Not much. We were in seminary together. He was a few years ahead of me but it's a small student body. We all knew each other. I highly doubt he would have anything to do with this. Besides he was at a meeting with the finance committee till 11:00. The local police already talked to him. He came back to check on the church and lock up when he discovered the body."

"It would have been nice if they had thought to put that in the report," Jennifer said.

"Have you talked to Joanna recently?" Michael asked. "I sent our nephew, Dylan, a birthday card with a few bucks for his last birthday. Got a nice thank you note but no real communication."

"Spoke to her last month, but haven't been out to see her since her youngest, Monica, was christened about a year ago," Martin replied. "She seems to be very happy. Maybe third time's the charm."

"Well she must be happy with Jack.Monica's her fourth child, first with him. Four kids! At least she's producing like a good Catholic. What was the last one baptized as?" Michael asked.

"Presbyterian. But I'm working on her. The church has eased its approach to divorce a great deal lately. If she ever did decide to return, I don't think it would be a problem," Martin said.

"Always recruiting. You don't give up easily."

Jennifer was amused by the familial banter. She was an only child and often thought about what it would be like to have a brother or sister.

"Oh, Michael, this is new information. A fifty-dollar bill was in the poor box. The box was emptied around 7:30, prior to the finance committee meeting. It may have been left by the killer. They don't get many fifties here."

"Interesting. Guilty conscience? Send it down to the crime lab for prints. I'll see that it gets back to the church. I know times are tough."

They reviewed the few facts contained in the report and Michael explained the possible connection to the case he and Jennifer were working on. The discussion was interspersed with friendly banter between the two brothers about shared experiences from their youth. Jennifer had wandered off to check out the crime scene and take in the church as a whole. She was struck by the Stations of the Cross that were embedded in the stained glass windows and the dressing of the altar, noting the difference between the Episcopal and Roman Catholic features. The Episcopal churches she had been in appeared to be more austere in fixtures but brighter in impression. She wondered if that had to do with the philosophical differences between the two. The actual services were really quite similar in structure but the overall feel was somewhat different. She finally looked at her watch and made her way back to Michael's side.

"I hate to break up the family reunion, but we have an appointment with April Carpenter at one, Michael," Jennifer broke in.

"Okay," Michael said. "Doesn't look like we can learn anything more here. The CSI reports should be available at the office. We're scheduled to interview Lily Carpenter's sister. If you have a card we could leave it with her in case she's worried about her soul."

Jennifer looked at Michael. "That was a little uncalled-for, Michael."

"Ooh, I think this one's a keeper Michael," Martin injected. "That is, if you can keep a partner for more than six months." Turning to Jennifer, he continued, "It was a pleasure to meet you detective. Don't be too tough on him. He really has a good soul hidden in there somewhere."

Michael just shook his head. "Well, keep an ear to the ground. I'll be in touch."

Before entering the vestibule, Michael turned to face the altar, genuflected and made the sign of the cross. He was aware that Jennifer was watching as he did. "Old habits die hard," he said.

"I like him," Jennifer said to Michael as they were approaching the car.

"Yeah, I think I'll keep him," Michael said with a smile on his face.

Michael and Jennifer arrived at Lily's sister's on time. The house was in the Mexican War Streets neighborhood on the north side of Pittsburgh. It's a few blocks of gentrified old city homes with a definite Victorian architectural feel and lends itself to an artistic appeal. It was recognized as an historical landmark in 1975 and covered 27 acres. Michael's home was adjacent to the area.

April Carpenter wasn't much help. She had talked to her sister about two days before the murder. They had spoken about Marissa's behavior. Lil knew her daughter was, for all practical purposes, an 'escort'. Lily couldn't bear a less polite term. She was powerless to control her daughter and frustrated with the wall between them that she didn't seem to be able to break through. Lily had taken to drinking too much. She had had a few romantic affairs over the last few years, but nobody at the current time that

April knew of. Her favorite bar was O'Shaughnessy's Pub, a neighborhood bar on Lincoln Avenue about two blocks from Lily's apartment. Lil often went there on Saturday nights. Ted, her ex, was a real son of a bitch; abused her physically and verbally during the marriage, and a lousy father. Lil finally divorced him primarily to get her daughter out of that environment. She had returned to her maiden name while Marissa kept her father's surname. April doubted he had anything to do with the murders, too much of a worm to actually have the strength to stand up to anyone. When Jennifer told her that there was evidence of sexual activity shortly before she was murdered, April just shrugged. "Loneliness is a desperate place," she said. They thanked her and left a card in case she thought of anything else that would help and headed back to the car.

"It's almost 3 o'clock," Michael said to Jennifer. "Want to catch lunch before returning?"

"I'm not really hungry. Mind if we skip lunch?," Jennifer replied.

"Not at all."

"I couldn't help but think about what it's like to have brothers and sisters after watching you and Martin," Jennifer said. "I often wonder if I'm depriving Meagan of that family feeling."

"Meagan seems to be doing fine and you are a very good mother Jen. There is no way to predict how kids turn out. I'm sure Lily Carpenter did everything she could to bring Marissa up right, and look how that turned out. It doesn't do any good to worry about 'what ifs'. We kind of have to trust our judgments at the time." Michael was silent for about a minute, obviously pondering whether or not to say what he was thinking. Finally, he glanced over at Jennifer and said, "Of course, if you're looking to produce another child...."

Jennifer cut him off. "That's quite enough from you, Michael Davis. We're already walking a line with our little 'date' with the Mayor." She was annoyed with herself for her own thoughts about how much she might enjoy being with Michael. It was not the first time she had thought about it and she was sure it would not be the last. It had been years since she had been with a man.

Michael was grinning. "I don't have to worry about a call from HR, do I?"

"It wouldn't surprise me, but it won't be from me," Jennifer said. "At least not yet."

They had arrived at the station. "Well, let's see what awaits us upstairs," Michael said, as they exited the car.

Chapter 15

Michael and Jennifer felt the change in the atmosphere a good ten feet before they crossed the threshold to the squad room. Jennifer's first thought was that the ballet 'date' was a mistake but by the time they entered she knew that wasn't it. Deputy Chief Morrow was standing in front of Michael's chalk board. Without turning, Morrow said, "You've kicked the hornet's nest."

"What are you talking about?" asked Michael.

"The ballistics are back on the bullets, all six of them; the four from the Carpenter scene and the two from St. Paul's. They are a match but that's just the beginning. Both Interpol and the FBI are looking for the gun that fired them. The 9mm is associated with a sniper who uses a M82AI bolt action sniper rifle tied to at least two dozen assassinations both domestic and abroad. Two MI6 agents were killed with the 9mm after they tracked down the sniper. One FBI agent was seriously wounded here in the states, also believed to be by the same pistol. The 9 is also matched to a number of shootings here in the states. The girls were shot without a silencer and Father Costello with a silencer. Both the pistol and the rifle have custom rifling for more precision and the bullets appear to be custom loads," said Morrow.

"Great!" said Michael. "How long before they descend?"

"Probably tomorrow," answered Morrow.

Michael looked at Jennifer and said, "The circus is in town. Sure to muck everything up."

"I've already sent them what we have and the timeline on the DNA has been accelerated. Should have the results sometime tomorrow. I'll try and keep them away as much as possible, but you know how it is. I think they enjoy riding roughshod over the locals," said Morrow. "Oh. Jennifer, this was delivered from the

Mayor's office specifically for you." He handed Jennifer an envelope hand-addressed to Meagan Palmer, c/o Detective Jennifer Palmer. It was on Office of the Mayor stationary. "Anything I should know about?," asked Morrow.

"Not that I'm aware of, Deputy Chief," answered Jennifer. Michael could see she was flushed. He was sure Morrow could too.

"Friends in high places?" Morrow asked.

"My daughter is friends with his daughter," Jennifer lied quite convincingly, thought Michael. "They both take ballet lessons together," Jennifer continued.

"Wow!" said Michael, continuing, "That could come in handy!"

"Don't rattle the cage, Mike," said Morrow as he exited the squad room.

"He's a master of clichés," Michael said loud enough for the others in the squad room to hear. He then added, "Move on boys and girls. Nothing to see here."

Jennifer stared at the envelope in her hands. Michael asked, "Is it sealed?"

Jen checked and said, "No but it's addressed to Meag. Don't know if I should open it."

Michael took half a step backwards, put his hands on his hips, cocked his head a little to the side and made his eyes as wide as they would go. "Really?" was all he said. Jennifer responded with a scrunched-up face and stuck her tongue out. She looked down at the envelope in her hands. Since it was not sealed, Jennifer opened it. Inside was a piece of folded stationary containing four tickets to the upcoming Katy Perry concert. She unfolded the paper. The header read, From the Office of the Mayor. A short, handwritten note said simply, "It's a corporate box and my wife will be there to chaperone. Surely your mother can't object to that." It was signed Bill.

"I'll kill her," said Jen.

Michael just started laughing. "Smart kid you've got there Detective Palmer."

"What now?" asked Jennifer.

"About Meagan or the case?" asked Michael.

"The case," said Jen almost in a snarl. "And what did you mean about the circus being in town?"

"We can expect agents from the FBI to descend any minute. Well at least we now know the cases are connected but how does a professional assassin fit into any of this?" said Michael walking over to his blackboard. "It makes me doubt that it's the kid. I think we need to check out that pub the sister mentioned and might as well run Father Costello's bank records."

"I'll have someone start on the bank records while we check out the pub," said Jen. She picked up the phone and spoke to someone in the records department on the 2nd floor. The only part Michael caught was, "It's now your highest priority." Damn she's efficient, Michael thought.

"It's already 5 o'clock," Michael said. "What say we call it a day and start fresh in the morning with O'Shaughnessy's?"

"Sounds good to me. It'll give me some time to grill my darling daughter about these" Jennifer said, shaking the envelope with the tickets.

"Go easy on the kid. If you think about it, it was rather clever on her part."

"Can't help but wonder what else they might have talked about, Michael. Little pitcher have big ears. Lord, you and Morrow have me talking in clichés now."

Chapter 16

It was Michael's turn to be the second one arriving at the squad room this morning. Jennifer was busy organizing their notes on her IPod and merging data with Excel spreadsheets. She looked up at Michael and said, "I've loaded O'Shaughnessy's directions into MapQuest. Shall we go?"

"Will they be open at this hour?" Michael asked.

"I checked. It seems they have a breakfast serving."

"Hold our calls," Michael said to no one special in the squad room and out the door they went.

Jen noticed that Michael was uncharacteristically quiet all the way to the car. He instinctively headed to her car, without any protest to take his, and settled in the passenger seat without a word. He had been so jovial upstairs. She got in, buckled up and started the car. "I assume you can work this thing," she said handing him the IPod.

"Sure. To the pub," he answered obviously distracted.

"Michael, spill," she said. "What's bothering you?"

"It's almost a week since we took this case. Now we have a related case, the usual footwork, and not a single suspect. Not a clue, not a hint or even a hunch. And if that's not bad enough, it appears we've tripped over an international professional hit man and will shortly have a hoard of acronyms mucking everything up. Hot shots trying to make a name for themselves pulling monkeys out of their ass," Michael answered.

"Well it will all be new to me. But you've been through this before. That kidnapping two years ago, a couple bank robberies. You solved them. Is this really that different?"

"I think it is," Michael answered. "An everyday woman, a wild teenager and an old priest? Makes no sense. How can they be connected? Why here? Did you see the ballistic hits? An undersecretary of finance for an emerging African country, a would-be revolutionary, a Brit in the House of Lords, a Mafia under boss. Where in God's name do Lily Carpenter, Marissa Collins and Father Costello fit into this mess?"

"I had the files sent to my lap top. Maybe there's something in there to help," Jennifer answered. "We'll find it."

She spotted the pub on California Ave. A sign said parking in back. She pulled around and parked. There was a rear entrance, which they used. It took a minute for their eyes to adjust. They were in a narrow hallway rich with the scent of greasy fried foods. Apparently, the kitchen was on their right. The restrooms were on the left identified with pictures perpendicular to the wainscoted paneled walls just high enough for a staggering body to miss on their way down the hall. The hall itself opened up to a shabby, but pleasant room. The floors were old worn hardwood, probably oak, with paths sanded by years of feet scuffling over them. The center of the room was occupied by eight three-foot square wooden tables on pedestals of real wood shaped like balusters. The tops were also wood, not laminate, like so many today. Along the left-hand wall were booths that somehow looked very inviting. They were upholstered in a burgundy velour material, not fake leather, with the backs channeled. On the right was a long wooden bar with a brass footrest. Behind the bar were shelves for bottles and two large mirrors with the names of old whisky brands printed on them; the silvering fading as a testament to their age. The lighting consisted of single bulbs with green glass shades hanging from the twelve foot high ceiling. Above the booths, on the walls, were pictures of Steelers, Pirates, and Penguins interspersed with photos of the old stadium and the city in general. The overall effect was an old, very well kept, neighborhood pub. Both Michael and Jen liked the place immediately.

Michael walked up to the bar and said to the bartender "Nice place." His sincerity was apparent. "I was looking for some help," he said while showing his badge to the bartender. "We're investigating the murder of Lily Carpenter and her daughter. Perhaps you can help."

"I was wondering when you'd get around to me," said the bartender.

Jennifer had pulled herself up on a bar stool to the bartender's right. She smiled at him and flashed her badge. Michael was amazed at how her smile seemed to soften people.

"I'm Mike Davis and this is my partner, Detective Palmer."

"Jennifer," she said as she offered her hand to the bartender. The bartender took her hand and shook it and said, "Pleased ma'am."

Michael continued, "And you are?"

"Sean, Sean O'Shaughnessy, and this is my place. O'Shaughnessy's Pub. Lily was a regular and a friend. Anything I can do I will. By the way, you look more like a Mickey. Do you mind?"

"No. That's what my brother calls me."

"And Detective Palmer, Jennifer, you're a little breath of heaven."

It was instantly apparent to Jennifer why this place was still around.

"We're particularly interested in a week ago Saturday," Jennifer said getting down to business. "Do you know if she was here?"

"That the Saturday before she was murdered, right?" O'Shaughnessy asked.

"That's right," Jennifer confirmed. "Do you recall if she was here and who she may have been with?"

"Bet I do," answered O'Shaughnessy, staring at Michael. "Well, she came in alone but wound up talking to this guy. I didn't know him, not a regular, but they moved to a booth. Drank quite a bit and stayed till close. He was drinking Jameson's on the rocks; shame to water down a good Irish sipping whiskey like that, but that's what he ordered. She knocked off at least a bottle of our cabernet. I was a bit curious but then it wasn't none of my business. Looked like he was getting lucky that night. Didn't like him though. Avoided your eyes, didn't want to be looked at, but I saw him, saw right through him. Like I said not a 'regular'. You know."

"Do you think you could describe him to a police sketch artist?" asked Michael.

"Sure could but, you know, I been kinda staring at you. Didn't mean to be rude or nothing, but he kinda looked like an older version of you. Oh, hair graying at the sides and had long hair tied up behind his head, more wrinkles but still, a lot like you. Like a brother or cousin or something."

Michael was at a loss for words. Jennifer had never seen him rattled before. She jumped in.

"Do you think you could come downtown and work with a sketch artist tomorrow?"

"Well it would have to be in the morning. I can have Franky open for breakfast," O'Shaughnessy answered. "Do you have any suspects yet?"

"Well, I can't really answer that," Jennifer replied, "but your help would be greatly appreciated. By the way, did you know Lily's daughter, Marissa?"

"Trouble, that one," O'Shaughnessy answered. "I hate to speak ill of the dead but I threw her out of here more than once; trying to get served with her gentleman friends. She knew better to come in here. Hadn't seen her in a couple of months. God bless her sainted mother for putting up with the likes of her."

Michael still seemed a little rattled but managed to compose himself. "Well, we'll set things up for tomorrow; 9:00 am, ok? You've been a lot of help, Sean. Maybe I'll be back for a drink off-duty. I really like your place."

"Thank you for all your assistance, Mr. O'Shaughnessy. I'm sure we'll be talking again," Jennifer added.

"Please, call me Sean. Can't have a lovely lady like yourself calling me mister."

Jennifer gave him a smile. "Sean it is then."

And down the back hallway they went.

When they got back to the car, Michael stood at the passenger door and violently slammed his fist on the roof of the car. Jennifer, who was about to open her door, stopped and put both hands on the roof line and, looking straight at Michael, said "Is there a reason you're attacking my car?" Michael was holding himself off from the car with both arms extended and his hands on the roof line and looking down at the ground. Jennifer continued with obvious concern in her voice, "Michael, what is it? I've seen you mad but this is something else. Can you please tell me?" When he continued to just look down, just shaking his head, she said softly, "Michael, hey it's me."

Michael looked at her and started to say something, stopped as if he were gathering his thoughts, and finally said, "I fucked up!"

"Michael what are you talking about?" Jennifer was almost imploring. There was no question of how this behavior had affected her. The six weeks, now seven, they had been partnered together had seemed like six years. They had instantly connected and bonded. Michael had been an absolute rock. He laughed at her mistakes and gently explained what the problem was. He was affable and a great teacher. He joked about her precision, but appreciated its effectiveness. She liked the way he cared about the friendships he demolished when undercover. He cared about relationships. It hurt him to betray the people he had spent years setting up, because it was his job. He knew there was so much more to it, and still he did his job in the end. She had seen many things in him, or at least she thought she had, but this was new; she had never seen him like this. An electric-like pulse ran down the center of her back. Now she was frozen, waiting for Michael to act; to do or say something.

Michael took a deep breath, shook his whole , starting with his head rolling over his shoulders, then his shoulders, front to back; swayed on his hips and pushing his chest up, a twist to each side; it looked like a yoga stretching routine. Another deep, cleansing breath and he opened the door and dropped into the passenger seat. Jennifer opened the driver door and sat, put her seat belt on and started the car, but she did not put the car in gear.

"Michael, you need to tell me what's going on. How did you, er, 'fuck' up?"

"How tall was he? I didn't ask. Do you have the bill? How did he pay? Do you have any cameras? As soon as he said the guy looked like me my mind just went off on its own. I was Alex again. Afraid someone would recognize me. I was on my first couple patrols after returning to a beat. Was that Kate who just passed? My mind was just rolling over, tripping over itself. It was as if my identity was wandering. I didn't even hear what you two were talking about. Something about the bar, the fact the guy looked like me. I was lost. That has never happened before. That just can't afford to happen."

"Michael, none of that showed. You seemed fine. A little distracted maybe but fine. You set up the appointment with the sketch artist. If we need more, we can get it tomorrow. Anyway, I'm sure you just resembled the guy. If he thought you looked like him, what do you think he'd think about Martin? He still has the ponytail."

Michael raised his hand up to the side off his head and gave it a twist; thumb on his jaw line and fingers parallel to his ear. And then he was back to himself again. Jennifer put the car in gear and headed back out to the street.

"You want to try to catch those two boys at school? Hopefully we can cross them off the list. Not too many high school juniors that are also international killers?" Jennifer glanced over at Michael as he asked. She could tell he was almost back to the Michael she had become accustomed to.

"No, but one of them may have found a gun," Jennifer responded.

"Good thinking, Friday," Michael responded. "And why not shoot a priest hearing confession while he's at it?"

"Well at least we could move them to a different column on your blackboard," Jennifer replied.

"Touché. The school it is."

They drove in silence for a while. Finally Michael spoke up, "The confessional! Did we actually confirm that Father Costello was in the act of hearing confession when he was killed?"

"Well, I just thought... He was half in the center booth...No, I don't think we did," answered Jen.

"He had that thing on, the scarf; I think it's called a pall. Priests wear it to grant absolution. He must have been hearing someone's confession. The killer?" Michael said. "We may have an assassin worried about his immortal soul. I doubt he's in high school but let's see if we can cross the kids off our list." He was obviously back to his normal self.

"Michael, about before..." Jennifer started.

"Sorry about that. There is something swimming in my head. This killer just feels familiar somehow, but I've never had a case like this. And now the Feds are coming. The killer resembles me. What's next? These things come in threes and I sense it will have to do with me."

"You're over reacting," Jennifer said. "Maybe this business with the ballet, the Mayor and Meagan has you rattled. I tried to warn you about professionalism."

"Nah. The Mayor's no threat to me. He's a pussy cat; political, but no threat. My press is good enough to keep him off my ass. There are too many easy pickings if he wants to come down on the department. An affair would be small change."

"An affair? What the hell! Michael we only went…"

"I didn't mean we actually…"

"Damned straight we didn't." Jennifer was totally freaked out.

"Well that would be the supposition. Calm down. It's not going to happen. I was just saying if someone were to raise an issue that's what it would be. I know it's not but that would be the infraction." Michael was scrambling but starting to regain his composure. "And what? Would it be so bad if we had had an affair? I mean…"

"Just stop Michael, just stop," Jennifer said. "We're here."

"And what a long strange trip it's been," Michael quoted The Grateful Dead.

"Yeah, a real roller coaster. And I still have to deal with Meagan. I got nowhere with her last night; just a surprised and very excited teenager grasping some tickets and dancing around the room."

"I don't know; I think you should give her a gold star. That's at least five hundred dollars worth of tickets."

It was Jennifer's turn to slam a door.

Things seemed to be going back to normal all around.

81

As expected, the school was a waste of time. If either Judd or Larry had even viewed that scene there would have been a puddle from where they stood. Judd was a bully and Larry was a fawning would-be lover but neither was a killer. They also didn't know anything about the church. It seemed at this point Marissa Collins was a false lead. They had hacked into her phone. It would be used as evidence to convict Bennet of statuory rape, along with three other men whose lives were about to be deservedly ruined, but they all had air tight alibis for Saturday night and Sunday morning. The best lead they had was the stranger who was with Lily Carpenter at the bar Saturday night.

They decided to go back to the squad room. See if anything turned up from the CSI report from the church.

After a few minutes of snaking through city streets, Michael said, "About before..."

Jennifer interrupted him, "Michael, its ok. I know how hard the undercover assignment was on you."

"Oh yeah, but not that. About us; about the flirting. It's just my natural tendency to go to an innuendo when I see an opening. It's a guy thing. You know how it is."

"Now it's my turn," said Jennifer continuing with a grin, "Would it be that bad?"

They both laughed about her come-but she regained herself and added, "Michael, I really like working with you. I've learned a lot in the past few weeks and there's no question you are an attractive man, but I've worked real hard to get here. You have no idea how hard it is for a woman to make detective. I'm flattered by your 'innuendos' but we need to keep this professional, particularly around the squad room. I want to stay partners a long time."

Michael was silent for awhile, then said, "Of course you're right but you'll have to put up with some jokes around the squad room. The guys expect it, you know."

They arrived back at the station and stopped on the second floor to make arrangements for the artist the next morning. Michael asked to be notified when he arrived since he had some additional questions for him. Then they walked up another flight to the squad room. Deputy Chief Morrow was there talking to two gentlemen. It was hardly necessary, but Morrow called them over to introduce them to the agents from the FBI.

Michael looked them over. Short, close cropped hair, not one strand out of place; impeccably tailored gray suits, ear pieces hanging over the collar; carefully tied four-in-hand-knots on their school ties. He thought they looked like a male version of the Bobbsey Twins. They might as well have neon signs over their heads. He had to admit that the tailoring on the suits was superb. There was no hint of the Glocks they carried in shoulder holsters under their suit coats. Cops usually wore belt holsters and you could spot them a mile away.

Deputy Chief Morrow introduced them as Jeff Hooper and Alan Whitfield. They exchanged pleasantries. Finally, Alan looked at Michael and asked "Your board Mike?"

"Yep. I like to visualize. Jen has it all on power point though. I believe you already have that."

"We received it yesterday. Did you get the file on the shooter?" Alan asked.

'We received it this morning," Jennifer said "but there was no behavioral profile."

"To be honest, we don't have enough to produce one yet," Alan again. "We were hoping you had something we could add. His behavior here has been the first that didn't fit with a paid assassin. We do have a name, or nickname though. We believe he goes by 'Angel'."

Michael had been moving Judd and Larry to the 'interviewed' column on his board when he heard the name Angel. He spun around and looked straight at Deputy Chief Morrow. Jeff noticed the reaction and asked, "Does that mean something to you, Davis?"

Morrow had not made the connection yet. "Six years ago, I was undercover and broke up a gang that had hired a hit man named Angel to take out a councilman. It caused us to close up the investigation and roll up the gang."

"I think I heard of that," said Jeff. "Record number of perps put away; a few in blue, too. So that was your work. Nice job, Davis."

"Did you get anything on Angel?" Alan asked.

"Nothing" answered Morrow. "He never came back for the second half of the payment, nor performed the hit. Nobody saw him; nobody knew him. All we had was a phone number that went nowhere."

"Shame" said Alan.

Deputy Chief Morrow turned his attention to Michael. You could hear the hesitation in his voice as he said, "Mike, we have another issue. We got the DNA back from the Carpenter scene."

There was something in Morrow's voice that led Michael to believe that the third shoe was about to drop.

"Do you know much about DNA, Mike?" Morrow went on. "There was no complete match. CODIS turned up nothing and Interpol decided not to pursue the lead unless we had more to go on. And the FBI did not find a complete match in their database either. However, they were able to capture the base matches or familial DNA strands. They cannot do much with that on a national level. There would be about 3,000,000 or 4,000,000 matches on a national level and about 10,000 identified to individuals, mostly convicted criminals, law enforcement individuals, medical patients; those who would have their DNA on file. However, on the state level, that breaks down to about 430,000, give or take 100,000 in Pennsylvania of which maybe 20 or 30 would already have been identified and more than a 3 or 400,000 never tested. Familial DNA is rarely used for law enforcement situations. So far it has only resulted in one conviction and that was in California in 2005. There is a case currently in the state Supreme Court on appeal for unlawful search in Virginia. They found a couple known matches and used possible matches of relatives to identify the perpetrator. The verdict is still out."

"Are you trying to tell me we have to investigate 300,000 people?" Michael asked.

"No, Davis. There are 12 known familial matches on file in the state," Jeff added. "And you're one of them."

Boom! The third shoe dropped.

Chapter 18

Michael spent the rest of the afternoon with agent Jeffrey Hooper making lists of known male relatives, including his own, searching for readily available information in computer files both public, like Spokeo, Facebook, etc., and FBI files. As for Michael, there were only eleven that he knew of: his Uncle John, his Uncle Stephen, his brother Martin, three of Uncle John's sons, (Seth, Charlie, and John Jr.), John Jr.'s son Peter, two of Charlie's sons, (Charles Jr. and Aaron), and two of Uncle Stephen's sons, (David and Jacob). The only one he knew the address of was Martin. He was both surprised and embarrassed that he did not know the ages and addresses of any of the others. He had last seen his uncles at his dad's funeral. He knew their cities but little else. Jeff was busily listing information on the others, while Michael was filling in information on his relatives. It left a bad taste in his mouth. He was researching his own relatives without their knowledge. It bothered him not so much about his lack of knowledge about his cousins and uncles, but more because he was invading their privacy. It was undercover all over again. It all made him painfully aware of the reason this was in the courts.

After they had finished compiling all the known matches, 54 in all, they started eliminating names. Uncle John and his offspring could be eliminated because John was his mother's brother. The DNA chain would not be a match. The dead and the incarcerated went off the list immediately leaving them 39. Then they eliminated any under 16 years of age or over 70. That knocked out another 12, taking the number down to 27. Another 6 were in the service and marked improbable; 21. 12 were now in distant states; also improbable; 9. And 4 were in the hospital, leaving 5. They printed out the last known pictures of the remaining 5. Martin was the only Davis left on the list. The remaining 4 were three brothers; last name O'Neil, who had been picked-up in a brawl after a football game, and a David O'Brian who was an officer on the Philadelphia police force.

"Wow," said Michael. "That came down pretty fast."

"Don't forget about the other 246,000 or more that we don't know anything about," Jeff said. "Even if we allow for proximity, age, and health, it probably leaves about 30,000 we know nothing about. I'm actually surprised at how few familiars are incarcerated. It appears you come from law abiding genes"

"Nah," said Michael. "We just don't get caught."

"I'm not exactly the right person to admit that to," Jeff said with a chuckle.

At least he's got a sense of humor, Michael thought. "What's next?" Michael asked.

"We quietly talk to the 5 left on the list. But not tonight," Jeff said.

"Want to go for a drink?" asked Michael.

"Appreciate the invitation but we try to keep our distance from the locals. The company frowns on any fraternization. Muddies the water," Jeff answered.

While they were compiling their information, Jennifer and agent Whitfield were reviewing the case. Much to his surprise, Alan found himself referring to Michael's blackboard a lot. He realized that Michael was right. There was something compelling about actually seeing things in white chalk on a blackboard that helped you concentrate. It was more compelling than a computer monitor, or perfect little letters on a printout. Jennifer was carefully studying the hits attributed to Angel. She converted the times to a chart, noting the dates, locations and victims.

"It appears Angel has a conscience," she said aloud"

"What do you mean?" Alan asked.

"Well, all these victims seemed to be relatively corrupt individuals, except the Interpol agents, of course. These were self protection. Horrible," she added quickly seeing the look on Alan's face, "but defineable." She paused for a minute and continued "That's probably the connection to our cases. For some reason he viewed these persons as a threat. But why?"

"You know, I think you're right," Alan answered. "Something happened in that apartment that made him feel the need to eliminate those two. Maybe he talked in his sleep or the girl found something that incriminated him. Riffled his pockets or something. And something he told the priest, something he confessed, or something that gave him away."

Jennifer added, "He took the time to take a sheet from the hall closet to cover the girl. He pulled the sheet over the head of the mother. It's not in the record yet, but he put a fifty dollar bill in the poor box at the church; it's being finger printed as we speak. Do we know if the priest's eyes were closed?"

"I'm not sure," answered Alan. "There should be a photo in the CSI report," he said, walking over to Michael's desk for a copy.

About then, Michael and Jeff crossed the room to join them. "Your girl here," Alan started to say, but immediately saw the anger in Michael's eyes. "I mean, Detective Palmer, just found a probable connection to the cases. They were closed, Detective Palmer."

Jennifer sensed the tension and quickly explained her theory.

"Makes a lot of sense, "Jeff said. "Gives us somewhere to pick up tomorrow. Mike and I thought we'd call it a night."

Jennifer looked at the clock on the wall and realized it was a little after six.

"Should we celebrate with a drink?" Alan asked.

Alan was the senior member of this team. Consequently, Jeff looked at Michael and sheepishly shrugged his shoulders.

Michael just thought this was another pin in Agent Whitfield's voodoo doll.

Jennifer spoke up, "I have to get home to feed my daughter. I'm already late and she worries about me."

"Well maybe another time," Alan said. "How about you Mike?"

"My company frowns on fraternization," Michael said, turning his head enough that Alan couldn't see and gave Jeff a wink. Jennifer looked a little confused for a second but let it go.

"What do you think? 8:00 tomorrow?" Michael said.

"Sounds good," said Alan. He and Jeff exited the squad room.

"What was that all about?" Jennifer asked Michael.

"I'm not sure myself," answered Michael. "Jeff seems like a decent guy, but there is something about Agent Alan Whitfield that just rubs me the wrong way. How was it working with him?"

"I have no idea," Jennifer said. "I don't think he said five words the whole time. He did spend a lot of time looking at your board, though. He seemed mesmerized by it."

"Well, I think we should call it a day, my girl," Michael drew out the 'my girl'. "Oh, congratulate Meagan for me. You can blame me for your being late."

Chapter 19

Jennifer arrived at the squad room about ten to eight. Michael was at his blackboard. He had taped the pictures of the five remaining DNA familial matches to his board. Beside each was a post-it with a question mark on it, except for Martin's, whose post-it said 'no way'.

"Meagan wants to know if you would like to go to the Katy Perry concert with us."

Michael thought about it for a second. "Didn't the note say the Mayor's wife would be chaperoning?" he asked. "Who else did she invite?"

"Yes, I expect Diane will be there and Meagan has already asked Emmy, my neighbor Bonnie's daughter, to go with her, and me of course," replied Jennifer.

"Probably not a good idea much as I'd enjoy it. I hear she puts on a hell of a show," Michael said.

"Well it's a month away. I'll stall her for a while. Maybe you'll change your mind," Jennifer replied.

As Michael was pondering if maybe it was Jennifer who wanted him to come, Alan and Jeff came through the door.

"Morning everyone," Alan said. "We brought donuts. Where's the coffee pot?"

"Over in the corner," Jennifer said pointing to an alcove behind their desks. "Hope you have a strong stomach."

"Can't be any worse than they had at Courtland Express," Alan said. "They have us on a shoe string budget."

Michael looked at Jeff. He was nodding in agreement. "Try the Days Inn two blocks down," Michael said. "Same rate. Cleaner and better coffee."

Jennifer started to ask Michael how he would know what the Days Inn coffee was like since his apartment was only about five minutes away, but caught herself before anyone noticed. What business of hers would it be how Michael would know about motels.

Alan was studying the blackboard. Michael had updated it with pictures and names of the individuals who were left from Jeff and his work from the previous day. Michael took advantage of the lull to speak up. "Well, let's set the agenda for the day." After all this was his territory, his case and his partner. He was determined not to let these Feds take control. "Did either of you want to take a look at the scenes of the crimes?"

"Is there anything to see that the reports didn't cover?" Asked Jeff.

"Not really, the photos cover it pretty well, but if you're hungry I'd eat my donut before you look at the photos from the Carpenter scene. It's an appetite killer," Michael said.

"Hey Mike, why do you have this 'no way' post-it on this guy?" asked Alan.

Before he could answer, Jeff said, "That's his brother, Father Martin Davis."

"Well that could be messy," Alan said. "The clergy hasn't been the symbol of purity lately."

For the second time in two days the hairs on the back of Michael's head stood up. He really didn't like this guy. "The 'no way' is my prediction. A suspect is a suspect but in the interest of professional distance, Martin should be handled by you guys," Michael said.

The words were no sooner out of his mouth than an officer from the second floor entered the room with a piece of paper in his hand.

"We are holding Mr. O'Shaughnessy for you Mike. You said you wanted to talk to him before he left. Oh, here's a copy of the sketch he and Dave worked on. He says it's right on."

"Yeah, tell him we'll be right down," Michael said, dropping into his chair. "Jennifer, do you have a list of those questions we wanted to ask?"

Jennifer was staring at Michael and she was frightened. All the color had drained from his face and he stared, totally fixated on the paper in his hand. "Yeah, I've got them on my iPod. Are you ok Michael?"

Alan and Jeff walked over to Michael's desk as she was speaking, fully aware that something was seriously wrong. Jennifer walked over as well and put a hand on Michael's shoulder. She looked down at the sketch. "I'll take care of O'Shaughnessy. Be back soon," and left to go interview the barkeep about the details.

In Michael's hands was a perfect portrait of his brother Martin.

Chapter 20

Two things happened almost simultaneously. Jennifer returned to the staff room and two uniformed policemen knocked on the front door of the St. Anne's rectory. Jennifer could see that Michael was somewhere between confused and irate. Grace Kopeckney, who was the Vice President of the Women's Auxiliary, as well as receptionist at the rectory, shouted from her desk, "Come in. It's open." Very shortly, time would find Jennifer trying to calm down Michael and Father Martin trying to calm down Grace.

"Michael, I'm sure everything will work out fine. We would pick up any suspect as well. You know that. It's standard operating procedure," Jennifer said as motherly as she could muster.

"You don't understand," Michael replied. "There is no more we! I've been taken off the case. Morrow just called me. The entire case is off base for me unless and until Martin is cleared. He's assigning Jim Walsh to work with you for the time being."

"Walsh?" It was Jennifer's turn to get mad. "He's a chauvinist pig. How am I supposed to work with him? Every time I bend over he's either looking down my blouse or checking out my ass."

As mad as Michael was, he couldn't help but respond, "Well, you really can't blame him for that. If that were a crime we'd lose half the force."

"Michael! Not now. Wrong place, wrong time."

"Yeah, I know. I couldn't help it but, for what it's worth, it helped me regain focus."

Jennifer composed herself. "Where are Abbott and Costello?"

"Down in one of the interview rooms waiting for my brother. I'd feel better if you were there."

"Damn straight I'm going to be there," Jennifer said. "Anything special I should look for or anything you want me to tell him?"

"Just that I know he's innocent and I'll touch base as soon as possible," said Michael.

Michael had never seen Jennifer so mad. He chuckled to himself as he realized he too was checking out her very comely ass as she exited.

Things were very different and yet much the same at the rectory.

"We just need to speak to Martin Davis," one of the officers said in response to Grace's questions. She first asked if something had happened at the school, then is it about one of the students; was anybody hurt?

"Well, Father Martin," she responded emphasizing Father, "is in the library. He's preparing his sermon for the service at St. Paul's this Sunday. I'll go get him." She left the office and walked down the hall to the library and came back shortly with Martin.

"Martin Davis?" The policeman asked.

"Yes. What can I do for Pittsburgh's finest today?" Martin replied.

"We need you to come down to the station and answer a few questions."

"Questions about what?" Martin replied.

"We are not at liberty to say, Father."

"I can't help but to be curious. You're outside your normal jurisdiction. Does this have anything to do with my brother?" Martin asked again, very pleasantly.

"No sir. Detective Davis will not be involved in this. We're just requesting your cooperation at this point, but we can get a warrant if you refuse."

"And what would this warrant be for, if I may ask?" Martin inquired, now somewhat concerned.

"Suspicion of Murder," the officer replied.

This was too much for Grace. "You idiots! There is no way Father Martin would be involved in anything like that. Have you lost your minds?"

Martin stepped in front of Grace, who was advancing on the officers in a very threatening manner. "Now Grace, I'm sure it's just a mix-up. I'll go with the officers and straighten everything out."

"I'm calling the Bishop" Grace declared as she picked up the phone on her desk. "He'll put these jagoffs in their place."

Martin was almost laughing as he said, "Grace! Such language. You don't need to bother the Bishop. I have not done anything and have no reason to fear. Let Father James know where I'll be. I should be back soon." He turned to the officers, "Lead the way, gentlemen."

As they were leaving, he heard the key tones of the phone being depressed. Grace was going to ignore him and call the Bishop anyway. As they were getting in the car, Martin said to the two officers, "She's really quite harmless, but she actually runs the place."

About the same time that the squad car was heading back to the station, Detective James Walsh walked into the squad room

95

and sat on the corner of Michael's desk. Walsh was a classic case of the Peter Principle; after 18 years on the force it was either move him up to detective or let him ride out his years as a patrolman. His scores on the exam were high enough; he had a few write-ups for brutality and discrimination, but nothing out of the ordinary at the time. So 9 years ago he was promoted to detective. It proved to be a less than stellar move. He had cost the city over $5,000,000 in law suits, one for brutality and two for discrimination. The result was a detective who was functional but little else. He was just biding time till his retirement. Outside the job, he was a bitter, misogynistic, racist bully; twice divorced and currently single. He was an anachronism on a police force that had moved on.

"Well Mike, did you finally fuck up?" he asked in a smug voice.

Michael ignored the slur and responded instead, "Let me catch you up on the case. It involves two women and a priest shot assassination-style by an unknown perp who appears to be an international hired killer. The FBI has two agents working here, assisting us with the apprehension of the killer. You'll be working with them and my partner, Detective Palmer. They are down at interrogation waiting for a suspect to be brought in. Have a ball."

"Why are you not there? And how come I'm being brought in at this point? Not that I don't cherish the idea of spending time with Palmer. She's easy on the eyes," Walsh inquired.

"The perp they're bringing in is my brother, Father Martin Davis," Michael said quickly, adding, "If you piss off Jennifer, you'll answer to me. Understand?"

Walsh didn't answer right away but it was clear he got the message. As he turned to head to interrogation, he muttered over his shoulder, "Jeez, someone has a thin skin."

Chapter 21

Grace Kopeckney did indeed call the Bishop who assured her he would send an attorney right over and thanked her for the heads-up, but it was the next thing she did that wound up having a greater impact on the outcome of the case. She called Joanna in California. Joanna was no longer the flighty little girl who was lost in the vanity of youth. Her third marriage was a return to the real world. Her husband was a computer engineer, relatively successful and a good father to the three children that she brought with her, as she tells it. She had learned that before you can love you have to respect yourself and find someone who can share equally in that love. She was quite a different person than her brothers had known.

She was surprised, or more accurately, shocked, that Martin was suspected of being a murderer; Marty had been by far the most stable member of the family.

"Grace, have you had a chance to talk to Michael?"

"No ma'am. The officers said he was not involved in this but, Father had mentioned just yesterday that Michael was handling the murder of Father Costello."

"A priest had been murdered?" Joanna inquired.

"Yes, and a woman and her daughter. It's all over the news. Do you want me to send you the newspaper accounts?"

"No, Grace. That won't be necessary. It's been too long since I've been home. As soon as I can make arrangements for the children, and touch base with Jack, I'll come home. Right now, I'm going to try to get in touch with Michael. Grace, I can't thank you enough. Marty speaks very highly of you. I can see why."

"Oh ma'am, it's been my pleasure to work with him. He's kind of been like a son to me but don't you dare tell him so."

"Your secret is safe with me Grace, but there's another secret that it's time my brothers knew. It may have a bearing on the case. I'll stop by as soon as I get settled and I'll email you a copy of my itinerary. And Grace, you've been a great help."

Joanna hung up and immediately called Michael. The call went to his messaging service. She left a brief message explaining her plans and asking him to call as soon as he gets it. Then she called Jack to explain the situation. Jack had met her brothers at their wedding and Martin had been out to visit on two other occasions. He liked her brothers and was stunned by even the thought that Martin could be suspected of even a minor crime, no less a murder. He volunteered his sister to help with the kids and assured her he'd take care of it. He told her not to worry about the cost and that they could discuss it more after dinner. She went on line to make the arrangements and emailed a copy to Grace. Joanna was amazed at how much more it was to fly on the spur of the moment as opposed to planning a month or two out as they did for their vacations, but it was Marty; damn the expense. After completing all her tasks, she poured herself a glass of wine and sat at the kitchen counter. It was only 7:30 in the morning there. It had been a long time since she had had a drink before lunch, and then only with her friends on a day out, but this was different; very different. She spent the next two hours trying to figure out how to share a secret she had promised to keep eleven years ago.

Chapter 22

Martin had arrived at the station and was escorted into an interrogation room on the second floor. On the ride over he had asked about his brother, but the officers had maintained total silence. He was directed to a seat in the middle of a rectangular table facing a large mirror. When Jennifer, Jeff, Alan and Walsh walked in, he was laughing. Walsh asked sternly "What's so funny?"

"It looks exactly like on TV" laughed Martin, waving to whoever was behind the mirror.

"Believe me, this is deadly serious," Alan said sternly as he took a seat facing Martin. I'm agent Alan Whitfield, FBI. This is my partner, Agent Hopper, and these are Detectives Palmer and Walsh." Martin started to stand with his hand outstretched. As he did, Detective Walsh moved his hand to his pistol and Alan was spooked by the movement. "Just sit if you please," said Jennifer quickly. "Best to sit relatively still Marty. Some people are rather jumpy."

"You two know each other"? Alan asked.

"Of course," Jennifer responded. "He's my partner's brother. And let's keep in mind; he's here voluntarily as a potential witness. How about we take it down a notch?"

Before Alan could respond, the door opened and an officer stuck his head in the door. "Father Davis' attorney is here."

"Well show him in," Alan said in a disgusted voice. "The more the merrier."

A diminutive figured walked in the door. He was dressed in traditional clerical garb: Black suit, black shoes, black shirt with a white collar exposed at the neck. He appeared to be in his late fifties, early sixties, and in spite of his size, he presented a dominant stature. "My name is Father Brian Stein, Esquire, attorney for Father Martin Davis."

"Stein?" said Walsh, under his breath, but audible.

"Yes, we're not all Jewish," responded Father Stein turning and staring directly at Detective Walsh. "Undergraduate right here at Duquesne and J.D. from Harvard. And you would be?"

Alan quickly took back the lead. "He would be detective James Walsh. He and Detective Jennifer Palmer are both members of the Pittsburgh Police Department. I am Agent Alan Whitfield, F.B.I and this is my partner, Agent Hopper."

"Four against two; I like the odds. May I ask on what charges you're holding my client?"

"As of yet, no charges have been filed. We brought Mr., er, Father Davis in to answer a few questions concerning three recent murders in the area. There are some apparent connections between him and the deceased that we need to explorer," Alan answered, adding "please have a seat." He extended an arm indicating the chair next to Martin.

Father Stein sat down next to Martin. "The Bishop sent me to assure you're appropriately assisted, Martin."

"I really doubt that's necessary, Brian, but always good to see you. I can't imagine why or how I would be associated with these murders."

"Unfortunately, things are rarely as simple as they appear. Oh, and the Bishop asked me to extend his thanks for helping out at St. Paul's. He has already heard very good things from a few of the parishioners." Turning to agent Whitfield he continued, "Am I to understand that Detective Davis has been removed from the case until this association with his brother has been cleared up?"

"That would be correct. News travels fast around here. That only occurred a little over an hour ago," Alan stated with a suspicious glance at Jennifer.

In response to the look Whitfield gave Jennifer, Father Stein replied, "Deputy Chief Morrow called the Bishop to let him know. It was he who requested that Michael, er, Detective Davis be assigned to the case originally." Looking straight at Alan, he added "Pity. I expect you'll be in need of him so let's get this matter cleared up as fast as possible."

Jennifer turned aside and stifled a giggle. Alan flushed slightly and responded, "I assure you that the competence of this investigation is more than capable to handle this."

Jennifer, not for the first time wondered what it was about Agent Whitfield that made people take an instant dislike to him.

Martin spoke up. "What exactly can I help you people with?"

Father Brian added before anyone could answer, "And why would the FBI. be brought into this case?"

Alan reluctantly responded, "as to the Bureau being involved, the weapon used has been associated with a number of other murders, both domestic and international. That piece of information would be best left in this room. There is already more media involvement than we would like. As to the first question," he opened a file that he had in front of him, "Mr. Davis, er, Father Davis, do you recognize any of these people?" He laid three pictures in front of Martin.

"Please call me Martin. It would seem to be easier," Martin said while looking at the photos placed in front of him. "As to the two females, other than the pictures in the media, I can't say that I do, but I was familiar with Father Costello. We were brothers in Christ and he was assigned to the parish just down from my own. As you may know, I'm helping with some of the duties since his death."

"I believe there is a name for a priest that another priest goes to for his own confession."

Father Brian fielded this question. "You're referring to a Father Confessor."

"Yes! That's it. Was Father Costello your Father Confessor Martin?"

"No, he was not."

"Do you know of any reason that someone would wish to kill him?"

"I can't think of any. The father was a bit of an anachronism. He was one of the few priests that still performed the Latin Rite once a week. He didn't adjust well to the changes in the liturgy. He hung on to the mysticism and pomp of the church. He believed the emphasis was on the glory of God not the congregation. Turning the altar to face the attendees of the mass was a sacrilege to him. The consecration was between the priest and God. He used to say 'the old ways were the best ways' and he was entrenched in the old ways. He had a reputation of assigning long and arduous penance for absolution. His confessions were lightly attended but hardly anything to kill for."

"Interesting," Alan said, glancing at Jennifer. "And you're sure you don't know this woman?" Alan asked, pointing to the photo of Lily Carpenter.

"I can't swear to the fact that she may have been to one of my services, but I can assure you that I never knew her directly."

"I see," said Alan. "Do you have a passport Martin?"

"I do."

"Have you ever been to Italy?"

"Why yes. On three occasions."

"Would those dates be listed on your passport?"

"Of course."

"How about France?"

"Only once. I had an opportunity to attend a conference on the importance of parochial schools. I was a presenter. One of my trips to Italy was for the same purpose."

"How about South Africa?"

"No, I'm afraid I haven't had the opportunity, but I'd love to go if you're planning my itinerary. How is any of this relevant?"

"Bear with me Martin," Alan said. "England?"

"A fairly long time ago for a class at Oxford while I was still in Seminary."

"And how often do you travel domestically?"

"Not that frequently. Mostly for conferences related to the church and occasionally to visit my sister in California. What has any of this to do with these murders, if I can ask?" Martin inquired.

"I assume this is relevant to the international connection to this investigation," Father Brian stated. "Is that correct, Agent Whitfield?"

"That is counselor" answered Alan.

"May I have a moment to confer with my client?" Father Brian asked. Without waiting for a reply, he whispered to Martin, "Is there anything you can think of that would be a reason for them not to examine your passport?"

Martin replied, "Not a thing."

"We would be happy to have you examine Father Davis's passport if this would help move things along."

"I thank you for that. It will probably not be necessary at this time. Perhaps later," Said Alan.

During all this questioning, Detective Walsh was standing off to the side leaning on a wall. He was shifting his weight from one leg to another and folding and unfolding his arms. Jennifer turned and said to him, "Oh, for God's sake go get a chair, Jim. Your fidgeting is driving me crazy." Detective Walsh stepped out for a second and returned with a chair, which he positioned next to Jennifer.

"Just a few more things," said Alan. "Do you own any firearms, Martin? A rifle or a pistol?"

"No," answered Martin. "Years ago, as a boy, I used to go hunting with my father and brother; rather a rite of passage around here. I had a 30-06 for deer hunting. My father had a number of rifles and shotguns. He also owned two pistols; a 22-caliber target pistol and a 357 Smith and Wesson. On occasion he needed the 357 to finish off a deer that was wounded but still alive. We sold them after his passing."

"Were you a good shot?" asked Alan.

"Keeping in mind that pride is a sin, I was an excellent shot but I assure you, I have not had a gun in my hands since my father died. I hated hunting. I only went along to please my father and spend time with him and my brother. As I said, we sold all of the firearms and accessories while disposing of my father's estate eleven years ago," Martin answered.

"Do you know what a silencer is, Father?" asked Alan.

"Of course I do. Have never used one though," Martin answered.

There was a brief pause. Father Stein broke the silence. "You've yet to bring up anything that would indicate Father Martin is in any way connected to this case. There must be something else."

"In fact there is," said Alan. There is a witness who saw a man with Lily Carpenter the evening before she was murdered.

We have a composite sketch of this man. It bears an uncanny resemblance to you Martin. Would you be willing to stand in a lineup?"

"May we see the sketch?" asked Father Brian.

Jennifer took the sketch out of the folder and placed it in front of Martin, on top of the three photos already on the table. Martin studied the photo closely. "Is that what I'm going to look like in ten or fifteen years?" he queried. The sketch definitely looked like an older version, but the overall resemblance was uncanny.

"Or you with makeup. Besides, the DNA..." Detective Walsh was cut off mid-sentence by an obviously annoyed Agent Whitfield, who had shot out of his chair with a look that could kill, directed toward Detective Walsh. Jennifer put her hand to her forehead to shade her eyes.

"What is this about DNA?" asked Father Stein, his voice clearly indicating the seriousness of this revelation.

"We will also be asking for a sample of Father Davis's DNA," Alan said, sitting back down trying to mask the anger in his voice.

"I was about to ask how you came to associate this sketch with Father Martin, but it seems there is more to this story," Father Brian said.

"It seems that Father Martin has a familial match to the killers DNA. We discovered the connection from detective Michael Davis's DNA, which was on file."

"I assume you're aware that familial DNA is not recognized in this state, Agent Whitfield?" Father Brian said. "It could not be used as a justification for a warrant. The sketch might get you a warrant for the lineup but the DNA would not."

"It's ok Brian. I didn't kill anyone and I certainly was not with Ms. Carpenter before she was killed, or any other time,"

Martin said to Father Stein. "I'll be happy to be in your lineup Agent Whitfield, or assist you in any way I can."

"Martin, you're putting yourself at risk unnecessarily"

"Brian, someone who bears a resemblance to me, a very close resemblance, is involved in this. I want to find Father Costello's murderer as badly as they do. They're just doing their job. How soon can we conduct this lineup?" asked Martin, turning to Alan.

"We're prepared to do it right away," said Alan. "And a cheek swab?"

"Of course" answered Martin. "Let's get this over with."

Chapter 23

Michael was climbing the walls of the squad room. He updated his blackboard and went through every possibility in his mind. Nothing fit; no connections. If it was Marissa, why the mother? If it was the mother, why the daughter? And if it was either, why Father Costello?

The whole thing made no sense. And how did an international killer fit in? He felt like his brain was going to explode. He wanted to know how the interview with his brother was going, but that made even less sense. Martin gave up hunting because he couldn't stand to watch a creature of God's die. He remembered the last hunting trip with Marty and his dad. Michael had dropped a 6 point buck. He was down but the shot had lodged in the shoulder, not a vital organ. His dad led the way through the clearing to the buck. He said to Michael, "it's a beauty Michael. You have to finish him off." Martin held back as Michael took the pistol and put one loud shot behind the buck's ear to finish it off. It wasn't loud enough to mask the retching of Martin just behind a big oak off to the left. Martin couldn't kill a cockroach without feeling horrible. And now Martin was one floor below him being asked inane questions and there was nothing he could do.

Michael headed out the door. He told Higgins, who had the desk closest to the door, "if anyone is looking for me tell them I went home for the day." The elevator stopped at the second floor and it took all of his strength not to get out and go to the viewing area adjacent to the number two interviewing room. Instead he watched the doors close, seeming to take twice the usual time; challenging his will. He exited the building and decided to walk the twelve blocks to his home. He could come back to get his car later.

Michael had purchased a house adjacent to the Mexican War Streets section on the North Side of Pittsburgh, an historical area almost completely returned to its historical past. It was the area where April Carpenter lived. It resembled the brownstones in D.C. at Georgetown. Michael had purchased the place after his assignment in undercover. It became his hideaway from almost everything; his deceptive past, the police force itself, his guilt for not being there for his family when his parents died, his lost identity in general. He found great solace in refurbishing the place. He had set up a shop in the basement with an impressive array of tools. There he crafted moldings and casements as close to the original as his skills would allow. When he first moved in, he intended to redo the plaster work on the walls and ceilings but after two weeks of choking on plaster dust, gave up and hired professionals. After all of that was done, he refinished the floors in all the rooms, sanding, filling, staining and coating the old, now refinished oak with urethane. Over the last six years he had completed the living room, dining room, center hall and two of the four bedrooms. He had finished all the doorways and windows with elaborate casements and capitals as close to the original as possible. He built the fluted pilasters and ogee capitals of solid cherry on a table saw in his shop. He did the same with the dentil molded backboard and 5 and ½ inch crown molding matching cove moldings. He had accomplished a great deal, but had a good bit yet to go. He worked as budget and energy would allow. A ¾" cherry 12'X6" board had almost doubled in cost in just the time he has been purchasing them.

He poured all of his extra time into his home. In the squad room he would talk about this date or that fling, but in fact, he had not been with a woman since Kate. And, of course, he hadn't been with Kate; Alex had been. It wasn't that he wouldn't love to have a woman to be with but rather that he wanted a woman he could share his life with, whom he could be honest with. He longed for a woman who could forgive him for his treatment of Kate, who he had left to believe he was dead rather than face her and admit that in spite of what they shared, she was a means to an end. As mixed up as her life was, she deserved more than that.

In short, he needed the same absolution that Angel was seeking before he killed Father Costello.

Michael was in his basement shop setting his biscuit joiner to put up panels for the island he had designed for the kitchen when the doorbell rang.

"What? Are you running out on me?" Jennifer said in feigned anger as Michael opened the door. "Didn't expect the great Detective Michael Davis to give up that easily."

"Hi Jen, come on in. I'm nowhere near giving up. I'm just trying to figure out where to go next. Would you like the cook's tour?" he said with a sweep of his hand.

"Absolutely. Did you do all of this yourself?" asked Jennifer, captured by the beauty of the woodwork.

"Yes, most of it," Michael replied, "but don't expect much from the furniture. All of my spare money goes into woodwork. Let's start downstairs; I need to turn off some machines I left running."

As they were walking down the stairs to Michael's shop, he asked, "How did things go with my brother? Did he confess"?

"Oh yes. The public execution is tomorrow morning." That drew a smile from Michael. Jennifer continued, "He did amazingly well. O'Shaughnessy picked him out of the lineup but made the statement that he was much younger than the man he had seen. He certainly could not be sure it was the man he saw unless Martin had deliberately disguised himself to look older. He also said that Martin was shorter than the man in the bar that Saturday. Finally O'Shaughnessy said that Martin was the man in the lineup closest to the man he saw. I thought agent Whitfield was going to explode. The Bishop had sent a really impressive lawyer to defend Martin. I believe his name was..." Jennifer stopped short mid-sentence. "Is this your shop? You really are set up to do all this work."

"It's really just the basics," Martin said trying to hide his joy at impressing her. "A basic table saw, a planner and joiner to put up panels, a jig saw for some cuts, a router for others. Those pieces you see hanging on the wall are templates for the various cuts and shapes. All those hoses are to capture the sawdust. As you can see there are only the two small windows so I needed the vacuum system." Michael hesitated for a moment and then continued, "I find solace down here. It's my escape room, I guess. There is something honest about wood, something tangible and real."

Jennifer was walking through the shop, touching the different pieces of wood, lost in the delightful smell of fresh cut wood. She saw a warmth and artistry in Michael she had not seen before. It touched something in her she had not felt in a long time. She met Michael's eyes as if she were seeing someone for the first time. She wanted to hold him to her and almost took a step when Michael spoke up and broke the spell. "So who did the Bishop send?"

"Oh, Father Brian Stein."

"The big guns. Martin must be something special. I never much thought about the power of the church. They close ranks like we do I guess. Well in this case it's much appreciated."

"As I left to find you, he was on the phone with the rectory to let someone named Grace know what was going on. Then they were going to do a cheek swab and release him. You weren't in the squad room and Higgins told me you'd gone home, so I drove over to fill you in. Oh, and the best thing, Walsh is off the case. He blurted out the information about the familial DNA in front of Martin and Stein. I thought Alan was going to have a stroke. Right after we left the interview area to set up the lineup, Alan called Deputy Chief Morrow. I could hear him screaming about the incompetence of the department, blah, blah, blah. Next thing I know, Morrow came down himself and escorted Walsh away. There's not enough to charge your brother, and you're back on the case. He did, however, say you need to be cautious."

The doorbell rang again. Michael looked at Jennifer who just shrugged her shoulders. "This is more company than this old house has seen in some time," Michael said. He flipped some switches to turn off some motors and headed upstairs with Jennifer behind him. As they approached the front door, they saw that it was Martin. Michael opened the door and waved Martin in. The two brothers hugged while Jennifer looked up at the crown molding. Michael closed the door and Martin gave a nod to Jennifer and took a couple steps into the hall and looked into the living room.

"I looove what you've done with the place," Martin said with a drawn out accent and a wrist on his hip, sashaying into the living room.

"Knock it off Marty," Michael replied. "Are you ok?"

"Mickey, I'm fine. I've got the big guy on my side. What could go wrong?"

"I've seen stranger things happen, Martin," Michael replied.

Martin turned to Jennifer, "It was really comfortable having you there Jen. Thank you."

"If you recall, I said virtually nothing," she replied.

"Your presence was enough," Martin said. "So, what's up Michael? You're off the case?"

"I guess I'm back on," Michael replied. "Jennifer told me that they just didn't find you guilty enough. Got to walk on eggs until your DNA comes back, but other than that I still have a mystery to solve. We have a look-a-like killer out there, and at some point in time he was related to us. Any Ideas?"

Jennifer interrupted. "Michael, a bathroom?"

"Top of the stairs. You're welcome to look around if you like. I'm going to take Martin into the kitchen and put a pot of coffee on. Come join us when you're done."

They spent the next two hours in the kitchen trying to make some sense out of the puzzle they were all mixed up in. Michael had found some slightly stale Danish to go with the coffee.

Chapter 24

That two hour conversation was when the three of them broke the case, although none of them knew it at the time.

Michael asked Martin if he still took two teaspoons of sugar and a touch of cream in his coffee. Martin replied, "I'm down to one. Doctor wants me to cut down on sweets. I have to check in with Grace; let her know I'm ok. I tried earlier but the phone was busy."

Martin walked in to the dining room to make the call from his cell phone. Michael poured two more cups of coffee, cream and sugar for him, black for Jennifer. He wondered if the way people take their coffee is set while still at home and if it's really an inherited taste.

Jennifer came into the kitchen and took a seat at the table. "Where's Martin?"

"He's calling the rectory. Grace, the receptionist, is like a mother to him. Like he needs it."

"Michael, I can't go over how fantastic your work on this house is. I didn't know you were such an artist."

"You wouldn't say that if you saw the boards I butchered when I first started. But, you know, once you understand the personality of a board, it becomes easy; well relatively easy. The tools do most of the work."

Martin walked back in. "You're too modest Mickey, the place is beautiful. But you left a hole over here and there are pipes sticking up."

"That's for the island. The plans are in the shop. I was planning to put up the side panels when Jennifer arrived."

Martin said, "You mean she doesn't live here? I assumed you would have settled that by now. I can see you're crazy about her."

Simultaneously Michael and Jennifer exclaimed, "It's not like that!"

"You even speak at the same time," Martin chuckled. "Okay, you can both pretend for now. Anyway, Mickey, Joanna is coming in. She arrives tomorrow at 6:00. Grace called her to let her know what was up. She has something she needs to tell us that she doesn't want to talk about on the phone."

"Oh no! She's not getting divorced again, is she?" Michael asked.

"No. She has finally settled down for good I believe. You didn't make it out for the christening, but you would have seen a very different Joanna. She and Jack are in a good place. The kids are happy. She's lost all the piercings and fallen into a comfortable suburban life. Jack's had a couple promotions. No, they're doing fine. It has something to do with us; some big family secret. She's booked at the William Penn for two days. Grace texted me the itinerary."

"The hell she is," said Michael. "I have to call her back anyway. She left a message on my cell and we're playing telephone tag. I'll call her later and have her stay here. We can have a late dinner here tomorrow night. Jen, you can bring Meagan. I have a feeling this family secret may have to do with this case." Michael refreshed their coffee and they settled down to review the case.

They breezed through Lily Carpenter and Marissa. All three agreed that Marissa was a false lead. Martin wanted to know how he became associated with Lily. Jennifer explained about O'Shaughnessy and the identification of the last known person to be seen with her. Martin said something about lost souls looking for love in all the wrong places. Michael told him he could save the world later and explained about the familial DNA and the connection with the FBI. He also told him about researching their family members and how it made him feel like invading their privacy. He didn't mention the guilty feeling of betrayal it brought back to him.

Jennifer explained about the ballistics and connection to Father Costello. Finally Jennifer explained her theory about 'Angel' trying to protect his identity. "He covered the women and we believe he closed Father Costello's eyes," Jennifer added.

"That makes some sense," Martin said. "If he felt the need to confess and regain God's blessing, Father Costello would appear to be the perfect one to go to. He always said the late night confession at St. Paul's and attendance was sparse to say the least. The dear Father had a reputation for harsh penances and lectures about the sincerity not to sin again. Assuming Angel was at some point a devout Catholic, he might have been looking for absolution. If he in any way indicated that he had committed a crime, Father Costello would not grant it without him agreeing to turn himself in. The sanctity of the sacrament of penance would have kept Father Costello from going to the police but that probably would not have occurred to the killer. Although it's not commonly accepted, forgiveness requires repentance. It's likely he was raised in a very religious family. These assassinations, were they like people who could be seen as evil or bad?"

"Jen, you're more familiar with that end than I," said Michael.

In response, Jennifer walked over to the counter and pulled her IPod out of her purse, grinned at Michael and said, "I couldn't fit the blackboard." She brought up the file and they reviewed the known hits; a mafia underboss in Italy, an anarchist in South Africa, a human trafficker in France, and so on. There were a couple that were hard to call, among them Alex's councilman, although he did turn out to be corrupt in time.

"He sees himself as an avenging angel," said Martin. "Confession was necessary because of guilt. They were people who didn't deserve to die."

"If that is the case," Michael offered, "he may be on the edge of breaking. He murdered a priest! Now his guilt will only be magnified."

After some more banter back and forth Martin said he should be getting back to the rectory. Michael asked Jennifer to drive them back to the station to get his car and he would drive Martin back. As they were leaving the house Martin said, "I can't wait for you two to realize what's happening here."

Michael responded, "Oh, we'll get him."

Martin said with a laugh, "I wasn't referring to the case. I was referring to you two."

Chapter 25

One o'clock in the morning, Michael's and Jennifer's phones rang almost simultaneously. The messages were basically the same. There's been a shooting at O'Shaughnessy's. He's shook up but okay. Michael was there in 15 minutes. He waited in his car for Jennifer. She arrived about 3 minutes later. They were ushered past the police tape, ducking past the increasing numbers of spectators and, gratefully, the news crews. Michael was used to the crowds but it was a relatively new scene for Jennifer. Once inside they were greeted by Lieutenant Jim Doyle. "We have to stop meeting like this," Doyle said to Michael.

"I agree Jim," Michael answered. "You remember my partner, Detective Palmer?"

"Of course. Evening Jennifer." Jennifer just nodded while taking in the room. "O'Shaughnessy's in the booth over there."

Michael went directly over to the booth while Jennifer assessed the scene. There was a small circular hole in the front window. The bullet had passed through a promotional window sign for Guinness Stout. The adhesive sign is probably what kept the window from breaking. At the other side of the end of the bar was a shattered mirror, also a promotional piece for Newcastle Brown Ale. It, however, was shattered. The bullet hole had already been marked and the bullet removed by the CSI people. Opposite from the spot where the mirror had hung was a stairway down to the basement of the bar. Jennifer went back to the bullet hole and looked back to the window. There was a clear sight line to a second story window from an apartment building across the way. Officer Doyle, who had walked back with her, said, "We have a crew over there going over the place. Nothing so far. They're canvassing the residents now but so far nobody saw anything. The crew has already sent the bullet to the lab. Appears to be a 50-caliber rifle load but we'll know more after analysis."

"Thanks Jim. That fits the M.O. of our guy."

"But I thought the other three were a 9mm pistol?"

"The shooter is associated with both weapons. I'm sure we'll find it matches the profile," Jennifer said and turned to join Michael.

"Mr. O'Shaughnessy was just coming up the stairs from changing a tap when the mirror was hit," Michael told her.

"From the looks of it, the trajectory, it would have been a direct hit on the heart of his reflection," Jennifer said.

"As I was saying Sean," Michael said to the still shaken up bartender, "we would be more comfortable if you would take advantage of a safe house. Just for a few days anyway. It would be much easier for us to protect you." Turning to Jennifer, he explained, "Mr. O'Shaughnessy lives upstairs and doesn't want to leave."

"I can understand, Sean, may I call you Sean?" Jennifer began. "At least for tonight. Our crews will be here for some time and you'd be better off getting some peace and quiet, recover yourself. The media is going to be driving you nuts. At this point it would be best to say as little as possible. We can hold them off for awhile, but as long as you're accessible they'll be on you like cats on mice. We can lock the place up tonight. Can you close down for a few days?"

"I'd just as soon remain open. I can have someone open tomorrow, but I'm not going to let this close me down. The last time we closed for a day was my dad's funeral 23 years ago. I'll be damned if I'm going to let some asshole get to me. But I guess I'll take you up on your offer for tonight. I've got to make a couple calls and get today's receipts in the safe, grab some stuff upstairs. I'll need that window replaced. Damned shame; it's been there as long as I can remember. I'll need about 20 minutes. You know this really sucks. "

"Is there any possibility this is just some pissed off customer or a jealous husband or something like that," Michael asked.

O'Shaughnessy looked at Jennifer, gave her a wink, and answered, "a jealous husband? Are you blind Davis? Does this look like someone who could seduce somebody's wife? No, it's got to be about Lily's death. Nothing else makes sense. But thanks for the vote of confidence."

One of the officers standing behind the bar held up a shotgun with a 16" long barrel, commonly known as a scatter gun. "If the son of a bitch had shown his face, I'd have blown it off." O'Shaughnessy said. "There's a baseball bat back there too. I've held it up a few times, but never had to use it. Yet," he added. "By the way, that guy I picked out in the lineup today?" He was studying Michael's face.

"My brother," Michael answered. "For what it's worth, he's a priest."

"I thought so," O'Shaughnessy said.

"Which? A priest or my brother?"

"Both." He looked over at Jennifer, "What's a lovely lady like you doing with a job like this?"

"And what makes you think I'm a lady," Jennifer said to him with a wink.

"Can I get either of you a drink? I'm going to have one," O'Shaughnessy said seeming to recompose himself. "On the house."

"Some other time," said Michael standing up. "Rules and all that, you know, and too many witnesses. Lieutenant Doyle will take you to the safe house when you're ready. I'm afraid you'll have to put up with some of Pittsburgh's finest for a time. Sorry you have to be mixed up in this. We really appreciate your help, Sean."

O'Shaughnessy headed over to the bar and Michael said to Jennifer, "I would prefer he not know that we're dealing with a professional assassin. This could have been a real disaster. Luck of the Irish I guess."

"Martin would probably say more like the hand of God. Either way, I'm glad Angel missed. I rather like the old coot" Jennifer said.

"Yeah, so do I," Michael agreed. "Well, we'd best try to get some sleep. The rest of the day is going to be hectic. I have some stuff to do to get ready for tonight's dinner. Are you bringing Meagan? She can play with my Xbox while we talk."

"Are you sure you want us there Michael? I mean, family and all."

"Consider yourself part of the family, and yes, I really want you there. I think you'll like Joanna."

On the way out Michael gave some instructions to Lieutenant Doyle for the accommodations for O'Shaughnessy and thanked him for taking care of things. He touched base with some of the officers on the scene, personally thanking them for their work at this ungodly hour, asking them about their families and stuff. Just generally letting all of them know he respected them and appreciated their work. As he exited the scene, he ignored the press, nodding to those who called him by name, but basically just holding up his hand as a 'no comment' gesture.

On the drive home Michael thought about Jennifer. How can you look so good when you're dragged out of bed at one in the morning? And she was as alert as can be. One quick look and she had analyzed the whole crime scene. Amazing, simply amazing.

Chapter 26

Martin was the earliest riser of the three. He was performing the 6:30 Mass at St. Anne's and had promised the Bishop to help go over the ledgers at St. Paul's later in the afternoon. "No sense taking any chances. Stranger things have happened," the Bishop had said on the phone.

"You sound like my brother," Martin had replied.

"He may be a heathen," the Bishop answered, "but he's a good one."

After service, Martin returned to the rectory to find Grace in a minor frenzy. She was tallying up receipts for the week, preparing this week's bank deposit.

"Still nothing from our mysterious benefactor, Father. That makes eight weeks since we've had a check. I hope nothing has happened to our glorious angel. It would leave a big hole in the budget."

"Come now Grace," Martin replied. "You know the Lord provides." It was a pro-forma answer. Martin's head had just exploded in a totally different direction. Angel! What if our angel is the Angel? What if St. Anne's luck was someone else's tragedy? Could it be blood money?

"Grace, how long have we been receiving gifts from our benefactor?"

"About 6 years or so Father. Why?"

"I was just wondering. And have they always been checks from that same off-shore account?"

"Why yes, Father. Remember all the fuss trying to track down the source a few years back. Even the dioceses couldn't trace them bouncing from bank to bank. They finally just gave up.

Do you think we should call the bank? It's in the Maldives but I could try."

"No Grace; not yet anyway. I was just wondering."

About the same time Martin was entering the rectory, Jennifer Palmer was waking her daughter, Meagan, for the third time.

"I mean it Meagan! I'm not driving you to school again because you missed the bus."

"Fine with me Mom. I'll just stay home today."

"No you certainly will not. Get your ass out of that bed this minute or no Katy Perry concert"

"Ah Mom, that's not fair. They are my tickets. And you said 'ass'. You're setting a bad example for my fragile mind." As Meagan finally got out of bed, she asked, "Is Michael coming to the concert with us?"

"I don't know yet but you can ask him yourself. We're going to his house for dinner tonight. His brother and sister will also be there."

"Oh wow! That's great," Meagan replied. Her voice clearly showed her excitement. "What are we having for dinner?"

"Nothing, if you don't get a move on it. What are you going to do when you're a freshman and need to leave 45 minutes earlier?"

"What time are we going?" Meagan asked, as she threw a tea shirt on over her jeans.

"We need to be there at seven, so if you have any homework, you need to do it right after school. I should be home by 5:30 and I'll be checking. And if you think you can use dinner as an excuse, if it's not done, you'll have to bring it and do it at Michael's. Of course, I could always get a sitter…"

"Nooo Mom. I'll make sure," was Meagan's reply.

Jennifer broke into a smile as soon as she was in the hall. Mothers and daughters, she though, shaking her head.

About the time Meagan was finally getting out of bed, Michael was pushing the snooze alarm on the app on his phone. A natural tendency to procrastinate had led him to leaving his phone on the dresser so that he had to get out of bed to answer it. He knew that once he was up, he would not turn over and go back to sleep. Besides, he read somewhere that you sound better if you stand while talking on the phone. It was in some post about 'Ten Habits of Effective Speaking.' He was hesitant at first but had to admit it worked.

Michael dropped the phone in the pocket of his pajama pants, the only thing he wore to sleep in, slipped into a pair of slippers he kept by the bed, and headed down to the kitchen. He liked to sit over a cup of coffee and visualize his day. It seldom went the way he wanted, but it made him feel better to have a plan. He was thinking of the best way to keep Alan and Jeff from discovering he was consulting with Martin and any possibility that his sister's secret might have a bearing on the case when the alarm went off again. He shuddered slightly from the vibration against his thigh and pulled the phone out of his pocket, turning the alarm off. He was embarrassed when he realized that the sensation on his thigh made him think of Jennifer. Brushing that aside, he returned to the plan for his day.

First there would be the reports on last night's, this morning's shooting. Check on O'Shaughnessy and read the scene reports. Maybe he could find a way to send Alan and Jeff out to check in with Sean or inspect the scene. He needed to plan a meal and call it into Market District. He could use the one in Robinson and pick it up on his way back from the airport. Have Joanna warm everything and plate it while he makes up her room. Check the menu with Jennifer and make sure that there is something special for Meagan. Review the initial contact with Angel. Is there anybody from the gang he might be able to get information from; anyone he's forgotten or left out? Any thoughts of the gang, especially Kate, brought a dark cloud over his mind. Thoughts of guilt and betrayal tried to sneak in. This morning, however, he managed to blow them away.

He returned to his thought of dinner and got excited about having his family around him. He'd forgotten the warmth of family banter and was looking forward to sharing it with Jennifer and Meagan. He left the kitchen to take a shower, confident that he was as prepared as he could be for the day, and perhaps more importantly, the evening. He found himself thinking of Jennifer again in his shower and took care of that as well.

The soon-to-be-fourth member of the group walked up the ramp to a plane at LAX due to arrive at PITT at 5:47. Her only concern was how to tell her brothers that their parents had produced another son before they were even married. There was a third Davis brother.

Chapter 27

When Michael arrived at the squad room Jennifer was already there going over the reports from the shooting at O'Shaughessy's. She saw Michael enter and broke into a grin.

"What could be the best news you could get to start your day, Michael?"

"They caught Angel exiting the building across from O'Shaughnessy's and he's downstairs in lockup," Michael answered.

"A little less utopian," Jennifer replied. "Agents Whitfield and Hopper left word that they would be out of the office all day. They are running down some of the other familiars in the middle of the state. There's a guy in Bellfonte who has a problem with the clergy. His son was molested by a Catholic priest and he has posted some nasty things on line and another in Mechanicsville who has a history of threatening women. At any rate, we are alone for the day."

"I love it. I was thinking about how we were going to handle our little collaboration with Martin. One down, four to go," Michael said with a grin on his face.

"What do you mean four to go?" asked Jennifer.

"Oh, just a thing that I do in the morning. I sit over my morning coffee and visualize how my day is going to go. This morning I listed five things: deal with the Bobbsey twins, check in with Sean and let him know we're following up, go through the CSI reports from the shooting, plan the dinner and pick up Joanna at the airport."

"It's obvious you don't have kids," Jennifer replied.

"Problems with Meagan?" Michael asked.

"Not really. Just the usual. Teenagers don't like to get out of bed. And you should be prepared; she wants to know if you're going to the concert with us and I told her to ask you. She's extremely excited about dinner tonight. I hope you're prepared to handle a thirteen-year-old groupy"

"Oh, you can't be surprised by her devotion to Katy Perry?" Michael replied.

"What Katy Perry? I was referring to you."

That made Michael chuckle. "Well you can hardly blame her," said Michael, puffing up his chest and brushing his hair back. "While we're on the subject, is there anything she doesn't like to eat? I was thinking of roast beef, mashed potatoes, gravy and green beans almondine."

"She would be happy with Big Macs and fries, but that sounds great."

"What about dessert? I was thinking about cannolis or éclairs?"

"Éclairs. I prefer cannolis, but éclairs are safer for her. This seems a little elaborate. Are you sure you want to go to all this trouble Michael?"

"It's my party and I'll buy if I want to," Michael said.

"Very punny, Detective Davis," Jennifer said with a bit of a grimace.

"One more. I'm assuming you would prefer she not have wine. Coke, Pepsi, Ginger Ale?"

"Coke. The liquid type. You've corrupted my daughter enough."

"Coca Cola it is. Two down." Michael said.

Higgins walked in and sat at his desk. "Hey Mike," he called across the room. "What did you do to Walsh? He's got a real burr up his ass this morning."

"Don't look at me Jim," Michael replied. "You have Jennifer to thank for that."

"Me?" said Jennifer.

"Well, whichever of you got him out of here, thank you. He drives me nuts with his continual bitching. I don't know why he just doesn't retire," Higgins said. There were a few other heads nodding in agreement.

"Things ok with your brother Mike?" Higgins asked.

"Just ducky Jim. It appears he's in the clear for the moment," Michael responded. "Like any brother of mine would be a professional hit man." He turned his attention to Jennifer. "Anything in the report?"

"Just opened the file," Jennifer answered. "There's a copy on your desk. Oh, Deputy Chief Morrow left a message. Martin's DNA results should be back tomorrow. Guess there are some advantages to having the FBI involved."

"I still hope their car breaks down around Altoona and they have to stay there awhile," Michael said, sitting down and opening the file on his desk.

The report was pretty much boiler plate. Side door of the apartment building across the street was jimmied; window on the first landing was partially open; gun powder residue on the ledge but no signs of a shell. A guy in the second floor apartment was up watching TV. He heard a pop but not loud enough for a gunshot. Probably used a silencer. He came out to see what the commotion was when the team got there. They found two boot prints out by the rear parking lot; could be anybodys, size 11½. They took a plaster cast just in case. CSI was running down the make and model of the boot.

"No surprises here," said Michael. "I think I'll call and order the food."

When Michael was done with the food order, he called the central office of the Pittsburgh Diocese to see if there were any records of threats or complaints about Father Costello.

"Anything there, Michael?" Jennifer asked after he had hung up.

"Well, no known threats but a number of complaints about his disposition. They're sending over a copy of the file. Should have thought about that sooner. This case has me off kilter."

They spent the rest of the day going over what little they did know about the cases and potential motives. There were numerous reports that had to be filed along with time cards for this morning's overtime. At one point, Jennifer remarked that she had no idea how much paperwork there was when she became a detective. "They don't show any of this on TV," she said.

The only plausible motive they had was the theory about covering his identity. The O'Shaughnessy shooting fit that one as well. At some point in the day, Michael pulled out the old notes from the arrests at the conclusion of his undercover assignment to see if he could find anything they had missed relating to Angel. He found nothing and wound up bringing up unpleasant feelings of guilt and betrayal. He had discovered that reflections on past events always brought up what if's; a totally useless but unavoidable mental exercise. After a while the thought of tonight's dinner brought him back to the present.

About 4:30 Michael left for the airport to avoid traffic on the Parkway W est. Jennifer stayed till 5:00, putting the files back in order and then left to check on Meagan's homework and get her ready for the evening. On the drive home she thought about how nice it was of Michael to include them in his little family reunion. It would be great for Meagan to be included in a family dinner. Michael just kept surprising her with his ability to touch a place inside her that she had thought was long dead.

Chapter 28

Michael found traffic unusually light and arrived at the airport in about 30 minutes. He pulled up to the gate for short term parking, took his ticket from the machine and found a space in the second row amazingly close to the terminal. After securing his pistol in the glove box, he locked the car and headed to the terminal. As a police detective he could carry his pistol but he didn't want to go through the entire rigmarole of identifying himself. He took the escalator up to the main concourse and found a flight board; United Flight 102, on time, Baggage Area C. He looked at his watch. 50 minutes to kill. He spotted a "Fridays" across the terminal and went in for a short beer. Grabbing a seat at a window table, he started to look around. He actually loved watching people; guessing what brought them to the airport, were they coming or going? The airport used to have a more active buzz. People came there to watch the planes take off, to eat and to drink, but since 9/11 it had taken on a more somber feeling. People seemed more nervous and suspicious. It was still interesting to watch them, but they were much more aware that they were being watched these days; took some of the fun out of it.

After about 20 minutes he finished his beer and headed down to the baggage area. You used to be able to go right to the gate and greet the person you were meeting as they came off the plane but that went away with landside terminals and security checks. As he sat in a row of molded plastic chairs across from Baggage Area C, he thought about stories his father told him about getting to the airport 30 minutes before your flight, getting your tickets at the counter and being in the air in a snap. Within 10 minutes, they would serve drinks and you could even smoke. Flights over two hours would serve food at no additional charge. It was a little hard to believe, but he guessed it was possible.

His thoughts were interrupted by a rush of people entering the baggage area. He spotted Joanna right away and saw that his brother was right. She was changed and it wasn't just the absence of piercings. She had a confidence in her walk, head held high, eyes alert. He'd seen a hint of this at her wedding to Jack, but he still remembered her best as the victim; head down, eyes turned away, slouched over. She was wearing jeans, but they were clean and stylish, tucked into knee high boots. She had on a red turtleneck sweater with raglan sleeves, and a coat over her arm. She was pulling what appeared to be a new overnight carry-on.

Michael greeted her with a hug. "You take all that metal out to get through the screening?" he said jokingly. "Honestly sis, you look like a whole new person."

"I am a new person Mickey, at least to you. What's it been, 4 years? I grew up."

"So what's this big secret you've been keeping?"

"Real nice, Michael! No how's Jack? How are the kids? Just wham, bam, thank you ma'am."

"Oh damn. Forgive me. Of course you're right. So how is Jack?"

"He's fine. We can talk in the car but the secret is for over this dinner you have planned when Martin is there."

"Ok, sure. Fine. Can I get the rest of your luggage?"

"This is all I brought. I can only stay two days Michael. Remember I have four kids at home."

As they exited the terminal, Michael said, "You really have changed Jo."

As they exited the parking lot and headed to the Market District Grocery Store to pick up the dinner order, Joanna filled him in on how her life had changed. Jack had indeed been very good for her. The birth of her latest child, Monica, had really changed their lives. No more drugs, not even the occasional weed. She talked about how different the older three were now that they were in a stable environment. She had started yoga after Monica was born to get her figure back. Dylan had just started kindergarten and Frankie and Devon were taking tennis lessons. They had a great four-bedroom house.

"You've got to come out Michael. You'd love the west coast."

"Yeah, well maybe soon. Right now I'm up to my ears in this case and, unfortunately, Martin is too. We can go over that later. By the way, my partner and her daughter are joining us for dinner. You'll meet her later." He pulled into a parking spot as close to the doors as he could get. "How about coming in with me to help carry this stuff out? Oh, and if you could pick out some wine for dinner that would be great."

"You want me to pick out the wine? In a grocery store? How things have changed."

"Well I thought, being from California and all…"

Joanna gave out a small laugh. "Sure Michael, I can do that."

On the way to Michael's place they talked about Joanna's transition from free spirited stoner lugging small children to concerts, and living in communes and group homes to what Michael called a 'Stepford Wife'.

"It's not as far a distance as you would think Michael. It's amazing what the right relationship will do. I don't want to sound like a west coast loony, Michael, but it's amazing what you can become if you just take charge of your life."

"Well, whatever happened, it suits you sis. I'm really happy for you."

As they pulled into the driveway, a rarity in this urban environment, Joanna spotted Martin sitting on the stoop. She barely waited for the car to stop to jump out of the car and run up to him. Martin was already standing when she threw her arms around his neck. He put his hands on her hips and swung her around laughing and smiling. Michael realized for the first time how close they were and how much he had missed in his years undercover.

Around the same time, Jennifer pulled into the driveway and parked behind him. He stood in the doorway of his car and watched as Meagan opened the door and ran up to him to give him a hug. As he smoothed the hair on the back of her head, Jennifer came out of her car. She had a big smile on her face watching the scene. As she turned to look at Michael, he saw her as if looking with new eyes. He didn't quite know what, but he knew something had changed.

Chapter 29

Martin was handling the introductions while Michael was unlocking the door. As they entered, it was obvious that Joanna and Meagan had never been there before. Joanna stopped dead, looking up at the trim on the doorways and ceiling. Meagan was looking into the living room at the 60" TV and the XBox. Simultaneously they both exclaimed, "Wow!" Michael just grinned from ear to ear.

"You like it sis?"

"Who wouldn't?" Joanna said.

"Go ahead Meagan. The remote is on the coffee table and the games are behind the doors on the right of the box. It's wireless," Michael said. "Marty, help me get the food out of the car. Jen, could you show Joanna up to the guest room? It's the one to the left of the bathroom."

About fifteen minutes later, Michael and Martin were in the living room with Meagan playing Mortal Combat. Joanna and Jennifer were in the kitchen, opening and closing drawers and cabinets looking for plates, wine glasses, cutlery, etc. "Where do you keep your silverware, Michael?" Joanna called from the kitchen.

"Never mind" called Jennifer, "I found it."

"So how long have you been my brother's partner Jen?" Joanna asked.

"About two months" Jen answered. "But it seems much longer."

"Is there a Mr. Palmer?"

"My husband was killed over six years ago. He was a police officer; killed in the line of duty. Michael caught his killer."

Joanna sensed some discomfort in Jennifer's voice. "I didn't mean to pry. If it's something you don't want to talk about, I understand," said Joanna, who had just found a platter in an upper cabinet.

"Oh, not at all, but like so many things it's a bit more complicated than a simple conversation."

"Well, anyway, your daughter seems quite taken by Michael. He always did have a way with women. Let's get the table set and see if we can get the boys away from their toys."

The next ten minutes were a flurry of activity getting dinner on the table. Everybody was passing each other, getting the roast out of the oven, the mashed potatoes and green beans in serving dishes. They were all passing each other while trying to avoid the pipes sticking out of the floor where the island was going to go. Martin stood in the doorway enjoying the hustle and bustle of a real old-fashioned family dinner.

"This was almost worth getting arrested for," he said.

"You weren't arrested Martin, just a person of interest" Jennifer replied.

Michael was looking for one of the bottles of wine and couldn't see it anywhere.

"Joanna, where did you put the wine?" Michael called out.

"It's in the fridge," Joanna said coming back into the kitchen from the dining room.

"I thought reds were served at room temperature?" said Michael as he pulled a bottle from the fridge.

"Common myth," said Joanna. "Actually 65 to 68 degrees is the proper temperature. That's why they're kept in cellars."

By now Michael was shuffling through drawers. "I know I have an opener here somewhere."

And then, as if a storm had cleared, they were all seated at the table. Michael was seated at the head of the table with Meagan, then Jennifer, to his left, and Joanna to his right. Martin sat at the foot. Michael got up and ran into the kitchen and came back with another wine glass which he put in front of Meagan. He picked up the wine bottle and proceeded around the table starting with Joanna. When he got to Meagan, he looked at Jennifer. "Just a little for the toast?" He looked like a little boy asking his mother if he could keep the puppy he just found.

"Michael, you are hell bent on corrupting my daughter," Jennifer said. "Just a little; Martin can save her soul later."

Meagan looked at Michael with a big smile. "Thank you, Michael."

Michael poured the rest of the bottle in his glass and, still standing, held his glass up. The others followed and Michael said, "to family." Jennifer looked at him and noticed his eyes were just a little moist.

After they were seated again, Martin said, "Meagan, would you like to say grace?"

"Oh no, Father Martin, I think you'd be much better at that."

Martin smiled and began, "Bless us Oh Lord, for these Thy gifts which we are about to receive from Thy bounty through Christ, our Lord, Amen. And thank you, Michael, for this wonderful gathering."

And poof! The chaos returned. There was the passing of platters, clinking glasses and general confusion. Joanna had seen Meagan grimace at the dryness of the wine during the toast.

"Meagan dear, did you find that wine a little bitter?"

"Yeah, kind of," Meagan answered.

"It's a pinot noir. It can be a shock at first tasting. Try this," Joanna said. "Take a piece of the beef on your fork. Get a little of the outer crust with it and eat that first." She watched as Meagan did as she asked. "Now take a little sip again and see if it tastes different."

"Wow," said Meagan. "That's pretty good!"

"The tannins in the beef offset the tannins in the wine," Joanna explained.

"That's real nice honey," said Jennifer. "Now forget it for eight years."

"They can drink wine in Europe at thirteen, mom," Meagan answered.

"OK, next time we're in Europe you can get a refill."

"Michael, this food is fantastic," Joanna said, changing the subject. "I can't believe you got it from a grocery store. The beans are perfectly steamed."

"I really like them too," said Meagan. "But what are those pieces of wood in with them?"

Michael answered, laughing, "Well I guess in a way they are pieces of wood. They are almonds, a type of nut. They are very tasty. Try a few."

"Oh. I've had almonds before. I didn't recognize them sliced like that."

"It's called green beans almondine," said Jennifer. "So tell us about your kids Joanna."

"Well, there's Frankie, he is about your age Meagan. His real name is Francis. He was named after his father. He's tall and blond. He'll be a freshman in the fall. And then there is Devon..."

"Also named after his father," interrupted Michael.

Joanna shot him a visual dart. If Meagan caught it, she didn't react. "Devon is 10. He's really into sports and he starts middle school next year. They are both really good at computer games. My Dylan," Joanna paused and looked at Michael before going on; daring him to say something else. He just smiled and she went on, "He's 7 and a terrible tease, like Michael. A little over 2 years ago my husband Jack and I had a little girl. Her name is Monica. We're close to the ocean, and also have a pool. They are all good swimmers and Frankie surfs with my husband, Jack. You should come out sometime."

"Yeah, right after Europe," Meagan said, making a scrunched-up face to her mother.

During the rest of the meal, they exchanged small talk about daily life events, school, and the differences between the two coasts. After everyone had seemed to finish their meal, Michael stood up again and said, "How about dessert?" and disappeared into the kitchen. He came out with a fresh bottle of wine and a box. He handed the bottle to Martin and the box to Meagan. "Take and pass," he said reseating himself.

Meagan took an éclair and passed the box to her mother. Jennifer looked in and smiled at Michael. She took a cannoli and passed the box to Martin. Martin took an éclair and passed the box to Joanna who chose a cannoli. Michael took the box back and took an éclair.

"Coffee anyone?" asked Jennifer. They all said yes except Meagan, who asked for a refill on her Coke. "I'll put a pot on," said Jen, heading to the kitchen.

"So, what's all this about a murder investigation?" Joanna asked.

Michael hesitated and looked over at Meagan. "Would you like to play some video games Meag?"

"Yeah, I know. It's not for my ears." She looked at Joanna and said, "They think I don't know about the murders they're working on. The girl was in high school. And there was also a priest who was killed," she said, looking at Martin. "And my mom found out that a counselor at the girl's high school was having sex with his students, supposedly got the girl pregnant, but she had an abortion." She looked up and her mother was standing in the kitchen doorway. She was just frozen there with a pot of coffee in one hand and a can of coke-a-cola in the other. The table was dead still.

Looking straight at her mother Meagan spoke. "You grow up pretty fast when your father is murdered and you're only six." Meagan snapped to, as if she'd been in a trance. She looked at her mother, tears starting to form in her eyes.

"Meagan...how," Jennifer shuddered.

"Kids talk, mom. We read the papers. I'm sorry mom, this wasn't the right time." She turned and looked at Michael. "Oh, Michael, I'm so sorry. I ruined your party."

"Not at all Meagan. You can say anything you want to at this table." He signaled to Jennifer to continue with the coffee. "You are among friends here, and by the way, what you heard is correct. The purpose of this dinner is to try and figure some stuff out. I'm glad you spoke up. Keeping things in isn't good for people." As he was speaking, he had put his arm around her shoulder. Jennifer was back in her seat and holding her daughter's hand. Joanna had turned to look at Martin. He just nodded toward the scene across the table from her and mouthed the words "I told you" without uttering a sound. Joanna had a broad smile as she spoke up, "I think a cup of coffee would be perfect about now."

Michael got up and took the coffee pot from Jennifer and did the honors, giving Jennifer and Meagan a chance to compose themselves.

Michael sat back down and looked at Meagan. "We were planning to talk about some things that I'm not sure you need to hear, but if you'd prefer, we could put that off."

"Absolutely not," said Meagan, jumping up and picking up her dishes. "You guys go ahead I'll clear the table and wash the dishes. Then I'll go try some of your games. I think I've said enough already tonight."

"I'll help you clear the dishes," said Joanna.

"There is no dishwasher, you know. It'll go in the island if I ever finish it."

"That's ok. I don't mind doing them by hand. You can close the doors. I'm fine now," Meagan replied as she started to clear the table.

Michael got up and closed the door to the kitchen, stopping to give Meagan a kiss on the forehead. As soon as Joanna returned, he closed the French doors between the living room and dining room and walked over and stood behind Jennifer with his hands on her shoulders. "That's quite a kid you've got there. You've done a great job."

Chapter 30

When things had regained a semblance of normality, Joanna spoke up. "Maybe we should have let her stay. The story I'm about to tell you is an excellent lesson for a young girl. It's the one our mother told me just before she died. She made me promise to keep it a secret. When I think about it now, it also has a lot to do with why dad and I had such a turbulent life after mom was gone; why I was so anxious to get away from the house and you two."

"Joanna, you make it seem so mysterious. I was there most of the time, at least the time I wasn't at seminary. I didn't notice anything," Martin said.

"Of course you didn't. You were in your own little world; you and Michael, the golden boys, one for service to the church and one for service to the government. And one little harlot left at home staying out late, doing God knows what with boys; throw dad's greatest threat in his face every time I left the house."

This time it was Michael's turn to interrupt. "Joanna, what are you talking about? It's as if we grew up in different homes! I don't understand."

Joanna looked at Jennifer, "You can see why I chose to keep this a secret. Men have such a different view of life," she said, looking at Jennifer. She refocused on her brothers. "You two are involved in this case because of your DNA, right? It's somehow tied into your genealogy, correct? Why am I not a suspect?"

Jennifer spoke up first. "Apparently, the genes indicate the sex of the person. In this case, it a male familial gene. So you are in the clear."

"Thank you, Jen. I had a feeling that was the case. You see, my dear brothers, there is no easy way to tell you so I'll just say it.

You have a brother you knew nothing about. He was born about 9 or 10 years before you, Michael."

There was dead silence in the room as her brothers let this sink in.

"That's crazy, Jo. Ten years before I was born, mom would have been in high school."

"The summer before her junior year, to be exact" Joanna answered. "Mark, dad, was the father." A silence fell over the table.

Martin broke it. "But they weren't married until dad finished the service and college!"

"And the next year, Michael was born," Joanna added. "Dad didn't know that I knew but I could tell he thought that if he gave it a chance, the same would happen to me. It turned out to be a self-fulfilling prophecy. Luckily it was in the spring and I was able to finish school. Frank and I ran off to California and got married by a JP, which Martin has never let me forget."

"Maybe that would have been a good tale for Meagan to hear," Jennifer added. "I guess I found out tonight that she's more aware of things than I thought."

"But what happened to the baby?" Michael asked.

"I'm not sure" Joanna answered. "Mom went to a home for unwed mothers to have the child and returned to school for her senior year. She said something about an orphanage. It was the '70's. They still had them back then. I really don't think she knew. Grandma and Grandpa handled most of it, but I think she referred to him as Anthony after the patron saint of innocent lambs."

Michael got up and started pacing back and forth across the dining room. "So all we have to do is find an orphaned brother from 1972 in a system that no longer exists, maybe named Anthony and possibly a professional assassin; piece of cake."

"No thank you, Mickey. Not on top of the éclair," Martin answered. "But I think I could use a refill on the wine."

Michael flashed a phony smile and passed the second bottle of wine, holding it up to the light as he handed it to Joanna. There wasn't much left in the bottle. "I think I have a bottle of Cabernet in the kitchen. It just may be a three-bottle-night." Jennifer followed him into the kitchen. Michael noticed that Meagan had done a great job on the dishes as he was opening the wine. Jennifer asked, "Well, where do we go from here?"

"We need to find Anthony, if that's the name that stuck. I'm afraid we'll have to involve Jeff and Alan. Adoption files are sealed and we need a warrant. They can get the records we need much quicker than we can."

"How are you handling the news that your parents had feet of clay?"

"I'm not sure. It hasn't settled in yet. How are you going to handle Meagan's growth spurt?"

They looked at each other and started laughing. They were still laughing as they entered the dining room. Martin and Joanna looked first at them and then each other and also broke into laughter. They were all just getting composed as the doors to the dining room opened and Meagan stuck her head in and said "What's going on in here?" At that, they broke into another round of uncontrollable laughter.

Michael came out of it long enough to say "It's just shock my dear," as he waved Meagan into the room. "We all realized how serious we were all being and it struck someone funny. They started laughing and the next thing you know we were all laughing. Life has a way of making you feel silly sometimes. Come on in if you want. Is that ok with everyone?" Michael asked. Nods all around.

Michael went on "We were talking about a high school girl getting pregnant. I'm sure that you're aware that it happens."

"Was it that girl that was killed?" asked Meagan.

"No. In fact it was our mother. Only Jo knew and she thought it was time Father Martin and I knew about it. It might have some bearing on the case your mother and I are working on, and I can't go into details but it led into some things about our family. Our minds were so confused with new information, they decided they couldn't handle any more and decided it was time for a good laugh. Once you start, it's hard to stop. Haven't you ever had a laughing jag with your friends?"

"I thought it was something you grew out of," Meagan said.

"I hope we never get to the stage when we can't laugh" Martin said.

Joanna jumped in, "Life can get very complicated if you get pregnant in high school, Meagan. It's not really something to laugh at."

"See Mom, I told you I should go on the pill," Meagan spouted out.

Jennifer turned beet red and that caused another fit of laughter, only this time Meagan was laughing along with the rest of them.

Martin finally stood up and said, "Come on Meag; let's see if you can beat me at Mortal Combat." Martin picked up his wine and headed into the living room.

"Just for a little bit. We need to call it a night soon" Jennifer called after her.

Michael looked at Jennifer, "There's not anything more we can do till tomorrow. I think I'll go watch the death match."

Joanna said to Jennifer, "I think I'll step out on the porch for a cigarette. Care to accompany me?"

"I quit a while ago, but I think I could use one tonight."

Chapter 31

"God, I'd forgotten how good these taste," Jennifer said. "I gave them up when I was pregnant, thirteen years ago. Never went back."

"I never gave up anything with my first three, except their fathers. Thank god I found Jack. Frank, my first husband, was 19 and I was 18. After the baby was born we took off for California in a VW Beetle; joined a commune. Frankie believed in sharing, mostly himself. I took off with Devon, a guitar player with a local band. I got a divorce in Vegas during a weeklong gig, and Devon and I got married the next day. We found an apartment in the Barrio in LA, where I had another kid, Devon, and shortly after another named Dylan. I raised the kids as he went out on month long tours. I was working as a waitress, at night, while a neighbor watched the kids. That's where I met Jack. He was a fledgling computer engineer. For the first time in my life, I understood what love was supposed to be. We took it slow, but after about a year, Devon and I divorced and he gave up custody of his sons. Jack adopted them right away. It took two more years to find Frankie and he just wanted $1000.00 to give up his rights to little Frankie. Jack adopted him as well. It's been a fairy tale ever since. Maybe I should tell Meagan that little story; sort of a scared straight experience."

"Obviously, I'm going to need to confront Meagan's feelings about her father's death. Maybe I need to confront mine as well."

"What do you mean?" Joanna asked.

"I don't know why, but I'm going to tell you something I have never told anyone. Maybe it's just a night for confessions," said Jen. "I was a junior at the University of Pittsburgh, majoring in Psychology, when I got pregnant with Meagan. College was enough of a financial struggle before, but now seemed an insurmountable mountain. I'd been working two jobs just to make ends meet and the courses kept getting more time-consuming as I advanced in levels. There was a practicum the next semester which meant giving up at least one job. Jim and I had met when I was a freshman and just seemed to connect. He was a year ahead of me and on a full athletic scholarship for football as a wide receiver. He was majoring in law enforcement and a cadet in ROTC. In his junior year, a hit took out his left knee. The university patched him up, but his scholarship was gone for his senior year. Luckily ROTC covered most of the expenses for his final year and while the knee ended football it left him healthy enough for the military. He would graduate a Second Lieutenant with a two-year commitment to the U. S. Army. Could be worse."

"Basically, we were two kids living in an artificial environment, facing decisions that would set us on life's path. Jim was excited about the prospect of being a husband and father. He was going to be an Army officer with a beautiful wife and a kid. It was his idea of what life was supposed to be. I was far less certain. I wasn't at all sure that playing house in school would transfer well to being a mother and military wife. Jim had a couple of ROTC friends who were married with a child living off campus. When we got together I always felt like odd man out. The guys would go off by themselves and get drunk and talk sports or military stuff; the wives would gather in the kitchen and complain about money and their kids. I wanted to believe that it would be different with Jim, but I'd taken enough psych courses to suppress my doubts. As my pregnancy progressed, I surrendered to Jim's dream. I dropped out of school but kept working two jobs."

"We were married in the campus chapel with a full military guard and both families attending. I was just short of six months pregnant. The reception was held at a banquet room at The Soldiers and Sailors Memorial adjacent to the campus. It was a beautiful ceremony, hardly indicative of life at Fort Dix that followed. Meagan was born on base that fall. We had settled into a tidy apartment on base. The décor was a combination of family hand-me-downs and IKEA. I never felt so alone in my life. I thanked God everyday for Meagan. She was the only thing keeping me sane. Jim was totally obsessed with his training and I didn't feel like he was there even when we were together. It was obvious he loved our daughter but he was of little help in her care. I made a few friends, but it seemed that as soon as I got close, they were off to another assignment. To make matters worse, Jim wasn't happy. He felt his superiors were idiots whose mission in life was to make his life miserable. I was hopeful when Jim announced that when his two years were up, he was getting out. It meant an additional commitment to the reserves but he just wanted out."

"Two years later we were back in Pittsburgh and Jim enrolled in the police academy. Life was much more comfortable and I managed to take enough classes to get my diploma in psychology. My family was close and fawned over Meagan. Jim was in a better mood. We had both reconnected with old friends. Times were still tough financially, but we got by with working part time jobs and my college loans were in deferment. Some of the old romance was returning to our marriage."

"Within a year Jim was hired as a Pittsburgh policeman and we had moved into a small house in the Millvale area and I settled into the role of a policeman's wife. After a while, however, Jim fell into his old habits; going out for drinks with the guys after his shift, coming home later and later from work. Any time I brought up the subject of his drinking, he became argumentative and moody. In intimate moments he would take care of his own needs and roll over and go to sleep. It became more of an obligation than shared activity and I avoided it whenever possible. It seemed the more I withdrew from sex the moodier he became and the more he drank. He was still attentive to his daughter and played with her when he was around but he was around less and less. The loneliness of Fort Dix returned. It only got worse over the next two years as Meagan turned six and I had had all I could take. I was a preparing to leave him about the same time I heard that knock on the door."

"In the next few months I found a strange attraction to the police department. They were extremely kind to me after the incident with Jim. They were incredibly supportive in so many ways. During the time Jim was in the hospital, I found meals left on the doorstep, officers and their wives volunteering to babysit, invitations to social events, even a fundraiser for Jim and our family. The connection stuck and when I was facing an uncertain future, the department seemed a natural fit. I entered the academy and excelled. For the first time in ages I found my studies in psychology a valuable skill. After graduation from the academy I was hired by the Pittsburgh Police Force. I thrived as a police officer and excelled as an interrogator. Within four years I was promoted to Detective. My first assignment was to partner with Michael, the very officer who had caught my husband's killer. I was warned that he was tough to work with. He has a reputation as a loner and had already been through two partners who had requested transfers. And here I am, unloading on his sister."

"You know what Jen?, Michael had it right. We're all family here. It took you longer to rebel, but we're both finally where we belong. You want another cigarette?"

"No. One was enough. Don't want to renew the acquaintance and certainly don't want to give Meagan an excuse."

"Fair enough. Let's go join the party. Maybe we can keep my brothers from corrupting your daughter any further. They grow up too fast on their own."

It took another hour for pleasantries and goodbyes. Michael and Joanna finished the open bottle of wine as they made up her room. Most of the small talk was about how sorry they were that they'd been missing from each other's lives for so long and promises to be closer in the future. In the back of Michaels mind, was how much his time undercover had really cost him. He couldn't get past the idea that it was just another relationship he had somehow betrayed without even realizing it until now. He finally drifted into sleep about one thirty in the morning.

Chapter 32

Friday, May 11, 2018; 3:11 am.

Michael woke with a start. He was in the middle of an extremely x-rated dream involving Jennifer and sat bolt upright. His first thought was that Meagan was knocking at the door, but quickly realized that it was his phone ringing. He got out of bed and picked up his phone on the dresser. Third time this week, he thought, it's a plot. He looked at the time and the caller. It was a little after 3:00 a.m. and the caller was Martin. "Martin! What the hell? It's 3 in the morning. Are you alright?"

"I'm fine Mickey but I thought I should call you. There was a fire at the convent this evening."

Before he could get anything else out, Michael interrupted: "I can be there in 15 minutes. Is everybody ok?"

"Everybody's fine. The fire is already out. But Mickey, it was limited to the basement. An accelerant was used. The only thing damaged were the records from the old orphanage that the good sisters ran until 1985. The sprinklers came on. There may be some salvage but I'm not sure. I convinced the local police to take the remains to your precinct."

"Good thinking Martin. I'll sic the feds on them and be out in the morning to check out the scene and talk to the sisters. Maybe one of them remembers a kid that looked like you."

"Oh Michael, tell Joanna to move the plans up to ten. I need some sleep. James is going to cover the 6:30 mass for me."

"Better yet, I'll bring her out with Jen and me. And Marty, keep alert. We don't know how desperate Angel might be."

"Will do. Try to get some sleep, my brother."

Chapter 33

Michael's alarm went off at 7:30 a.m. and for the second time this morning he bolted from his bed to the dresser to turn it off. He was fairly groggy but was immediately perked up by the smell of coffee wafting up the stairs. "Ah, Joanna," he thought. He threw on a robe and headed down to the kitchen. A steaming cup of coffee with cream and sugar was waiting for him at the table and Joanna was standing by the stove.

"Two questions," she said. "Do you still prefer sunny side up and what the hell was that uproar earlier this morning?" She opened the oven door and the smell of bacon overwhelmed his senses.

"Yes, and Martin," Michael replied. "There was a fire at the convent last night; arson. He was calling to fill me in."

"Wow! You're the fire department too? What would this city do without you?"

"The fire was set directly on top of the old records from the Parish orphanage that shut down in '85. He thought I should know. If you think about it, it was the parish our grandparents belonged to. It would make sense that they would be comfortable placing Anthony there."

"Was anybody hurt?"

"No. The sprinklers controlled the spread. He's having what's left of the records sent to the precinct."

"Our mysterious brother?"

"That's my guess. Oh, change of plans. I'm heading into the office, after a shower, and then up to St. Anne's to check out the scene and interview a few of the Sisters. I'll pick you up and take you to Martin. Should be around 10:00 or 10:30. Sound ok?"

"Sounds good to me," Joanna answered as she was taking the bacon out of the oven.

"Hell, if you do this every morning, you can stay here forever, Jo."

"This is heaven. Try getting a husband and three kids out the door and spending the rest of your day with a two-year-old attached to your hip. This is a vacation," she said as she buttered four slices of toast, plated the eggs and added three strips of bacon to each plate. She put one plate in front of Michael and added, "do you need anything else before I sit down?"

"Yeah, someone to do this every day," Michael answered.

"Anyone in mind?" Joanna said with a grin. "Child already included?"

"I get enough of that from Marty. I don't need it from you too," Said Michael. "We're just partners. We hardly know each other."

"Hey, I don't care if you're bonking her in the back of a patrol car," Joanna retorted.

"You kiss your kids with that mouth?" Michael replied.

"On a different subject, "Joanna said, "do you really believe that we have a murderer for a brother?"

"It's a distinct possibility, even a probability, given the DNA and family resemblance. You should see the artist"s sketch of the perp. It sent chills down my back. And now the fire at the orphanage connected to our parent's church? Admittedly circumstantial but pretty compelling. We know nothing about his past. It's that nature versus nurture thing. More up Jennifer's level of expertise than mine."

"Well I hope it turns out to be wrong. I'll clean up here and get packed up: be ready when you get back. Michael, your place is beautiful. I can see it is a labor of love. Maybe it needs someone else to share it with. Take it from your little sister; when you find true love, grab it and hold on tight. I wasted too much time learning how important it is."

Michael got up from the table, kissed his sister on the forehead. As he put his dishes in the sink he said, "It's been too long, Jo. I've missed you more than I knew. Right now, I need to shower and go meet the apparent would-be woman in my life, according to you and Marty, and track down a killer. Thanks for the breakfast, sis."

"You're ; and remember - you're no longer my oldest brother."

The thought startled Michael more than he had anticipated.

Chapter 34

As Michael stepped into the elevator, he heard Jennifer call out, "Hold the elevator." He pushed the hold button and was only slightly surprised at how her presence lifted his spirits. They were alone in the elevator and Jennifer was comfortable enough to say, "I really enjoyed last night, Michael."

"So did I, but wait until you hear how it ended," Michael responded as the doors to the third floor opened. They were immediately hit with the smell of burnt cardboard.

"What the hell…" Jennifer started but was interrupted by Michael.

"Someone tried to destroy the records from the orphanage in the basement at St. Anne's convent last night. Martin called me at three this morning. I had the remains sent here."

As they entered the squad room, they spotted twelve partially burnt wet cardboard file boxes with varying degrees of damage and equally wet papers inside them. There were two fans directed at the boxes attempting to dry them out. "You get used to it," said Alan Whitfield as he stood by the coffee maker with his partner Jeff Hooper.

"I apologize," said Michael. "I didn't think about the smell. Those are the records from an orphanage. We think that they might help us identify Angel. They were set on fire last night."

"I gathered that from the note your brother wrote accompanying them," said Alan. "What are we looking for?"

"Bring your coffee over and grab a seat," Michael said. "It appears our mother had a child out of wedlock about late '71 or early '72. Our father was the father providing a familial DNA. They were both in high school at the time."

"And you're just bringing this up now?" Jeff asked.

"Just found out last night," said Michael. "It was a family secret. My mother told my sister on her death bed with a request of secrecy. She heard about the situation with Martin and felt it was time to share the information. As to the fire, Angel seems to be ahead of us if my suspicions are correct. My guess is that when we brought Martin in, Angel realized that O'Shaughnessy was a witness, and upon seeing Martin realized that he was related, if he didn't already know that part. That explains the attempt on O'Shaughnessy's life. I assume that you got the reports on Thursday morning's shooting? If Angel had been in St. Anne's orphanage that would explain both the fire and the connection to Martin."

"Makes sense," Said Alan.

Michael continued, "There are some things I think you can do while these records dry enough to go through. My mother's maiden name was McGinnis. If you could find a record of the birth of a male child under her name or Davis, the father was the same as I said, about those dates and check for records of placement or adoption around the same time we might be able to find a name for Angel. Your computers are far superior to ours."

"And what will you be doing?" asked Alan.

"Jennifer and I are going to examine the scene of the fire and talk to some of the Sisters to see if we can find anything on that end."

"After a day of chasing down dead ends in the middle of this oversized state of yours, it will be a pleasure to work in an office," Jeff responded.

"Look at it this way," Said Jennifer, "you could have been in Texas." Jeff shot her a grin. "If you would be more comfortable, I can arrange a different office for you to work in."

"That sounds great. I'm not sure dry cleaning will get this stench out of my suit," Jeff replied.

"Alan?" said Michael, "sound like a plan to you?"

"Beats trying to go through those papers," Alan replied, looking at the stack of boxes in the corner.

Jennifer left with the two agents in tow while Michael called Joanna to let her know that they would be picking her up in about fifteen minutes.

Chapter 35

Michael and Jennifer picked up Joanna and her overnight bag and headed to St. Anne's.

"Michael, I just love your place. Next time I'll have to stay longer. You know, what you really need is someone to share it with," Joanna said after she got settled in the back seat.

"You made that point earlier, Jo. See what I have to put up with?" Michael said to Jennifer.

"Well she's correct about your place. And the three of you together are great company."

"And Jennifer, your daughter is just delightful," Joanna continued.

"Yeah, I guess I'll keep her. She had a really good time last night. It made me realize that was the first time I've ever included her in any truly adult stuff, other than the ballet with Michael last week."

"The ballet? With Michael? That must have been a new experience. I've never known my brother to be a patron of the arts."

"This from the girl who would drag her toddlers to Grateful Dead concerts," Michael shot back.

"It would appear that no permanent damage was done," Joanna responded.

Jennifer changed the subject. "Funny you should mention that. While we were at the ballet, Meagan managed to connive her way into private box seats for the Katy Perry concert coming up; from the Mayor no less. She has been waiting to hear from Michael as to whether or not he is coming."

"Oh Mickey, you have to go. Judging from her response to you last night, it would break her heart if you didn't," said Joanna. "I never realized you had such a rapport with kids."

"Yeah, well let's change the subject," said Michael. "How about telling me why you kept the news about a mysterious brother from Marty and me? That's kind of a big thing."

"Not fair Michael. It was a death bed request from mom and besides, I was only sixteen at the time. And then with dad and I butting heads all the time and you in some secret assignment. By the way, I never congratulated you on your success with that case. I understand it was quite the accomplishment," Joanna said.

"I understand. I didn't mean to chastise you. And by the way, Angel, the person we think is our brother, was the one who brought the whole undercover thing to a head. He was brought in for a contract on a councilman forcing us to close it down. We may have been able to tie in a few more people if we could go on a little longer but we couldn't risk a hit on a local politician."

"Jesus, Michael, this is one big mess. But hey, it brought us together. I've really enjoyed my visit. I've had to alter my image of you dramatically. It seems there are some sides to you I never realized."

"Michael, your family is such a joy. I've always wondered what life would have been like had I had siblings," Jennifer said, changing the subject once again.

"Yes, well it's certainly been interesting," Joanna said as they were pulling into the rectory.

"We're here," said Michael. "Come on and I'll introduce you two to Grace. I'll get your bag."

As they entered the rectory, Martin was sitting on the corner of Grace Kopeckney's desk. They were in a conversation about their mysterious benefactor.

"Ah, my adorable loving family," Martin said.

"OK, which one is Joanna?" Grace said as she stood up and came across the room to greet them.

"That would be me," answered Joanna, barely getting the words out before Grace embraced her.

"And this is my new partner, Jennifer, "said Michael.

"Hum! Maybe you can keep this one Michael," Grace responded, moving over to give him a hug too. "And Jennifer, Father Martin has told me all about you. How is Meagan?"

"Careful Jen, she's a regular boa constrictor. She'll swallow you whole if you don't watch out," Martin said.

"Why do I get the impression that would be a good thing?" said Jennifer as Grace moved over to give her an embrace, too.

"Well we should be headed over to the convent," Michael said. "Joanna, it's been great seeing you again."

"Yeah, just a little slice of heaven I'm sure. Take care of yourself Michael. It sounds like things are getting fairly dangerous. And you too Jen; I enjoyed our little talk last night. Take good care of my brother. I'm sure he needs it," Joanna replied. "Maybe Mickey can find some time to bring you and Meagan out to California some time. I know my boys would love it."

"I enjoyed it too," Jennifer replied. "And I'll work on Michael."

"By the way Michael, Grace and I were looking over the dates of the contributions from our benefactor. They bear a resemblance to the dates of the 'hits' from the FBI records. We may be looking at the same person, although I hope not for the sake of the Parish," Martin said.

"Oh, blood money, I hope not too," said Jennifer.

"Perish the thought," added Grace, trying to conceal the concern she felt.

"The path will lead where it may," added Michael, "but with the connection to the church, it's a distinct possibility. Well anyway, maybe we'll catch up later. I'll keep you posted; and Marty, as I said, be careful. Nobody knows where this may lead. Grace, always a pleasure," giving Grace another hug. "I'd tell you to keep an eye on the good Father for me but I know it's not necessary."

"Oh, on with you now Michael. Hurry and solve this thing," Grace said, getting in another hug. "It was a pleasure meeting you Jennifer."

With that said, Michael and Jennifer left the rectory and headed to the other side of the church toward the convent.

"And what little conversation were you and Joanna talking about?" asked Michael.

"Only one secret at a time, Mickey," Jennifer said teasingly.

Sister Mary Francis greeted Michael and Jennifer at the convent and introduced herself. "I'm in charge of both the convent and the school," she pronounced after introductions. "I suppose you want to see the basement where the fire was." She stood up so straight it reminded Michael of Sister Mary Margret putting a yard stick down his back in third grade. While she appeared stern, Michael saw the loving and caring nature he had experienced in his parochial school days from these mysterious black-garbed women.

"Of course, Sister, but first can you tell us anything about the Orphanage?" asked Jennifer.

"Well, let's go into my office then. I have some pictures of the place before it was torn down. All of that was before my tenure here," said Sister Mary Francis.

As they were walking to the office, Jennifer added, "I'm pleased to hear that nobody was hurt last night."

"Yes, God and the sprinkler system rained down on us this morning. No serious damage, just some smoke and lingering noxious odor." Sister said laughing.

Michael was just looking around. He had never been in a convent before and was pleasantly surprised to see that it was just like a typical home. He looked through one doorway and spotted a big screen TV, which gave him a chuckle. Having spent his elementary years in a parochial school he had his misgivings about the humanity of nuns. He thought that they might be living in cells or something. He had met the Bishop a few times and was convinced that he had a throne stashed away in some secret room in the diocese headquarters.

On the wall of the convent office, among the various pictures on the wall and the requisite crucifix, were three photos of the old orphanage. It was just above the convent adjacent to the school and about the same size as the convent. Sister Mary Francis picked up some papers from her desk and referred to them as she spoke. "The orphanage had opened in 1938 and served until 1984. The state regulations had made it too costly to operate any longer and it was closed. The building was torn down and the land sold in 1985. The revenue from the orphanage was added to the Parish's funds. I do not have any record of who purchased the land nor who built the current house that is now on it. I'm sorry to say that in the ten years that I have been here, I've never met the current owner. Sister Evangeline might know more. She is the only person left at the convent who worked at the orphanage. Shall I call her for you?"

"If it's not too much trouble," Jennifer responded. "I believe it would be helpful."

"Why don't we head downstairs and I'll have her join us."

Michael followed behind the two women, locked in his past. He discovered that he still had this arcane idea that you never question the nuns. It mystified him to realize how deeply indoctrinated he had been. He could stare down hardened criminals but quivered in the face of a bride of Christ. It made him feel foolish, but he couldn't shake off his past beliefs. He had questioned nuns before, but not in a convent. In his mind it was tantamount to questioning the pope 'ex cathedra'. Unless something made it necessary for him to speak, he was content to let Jennifer handle this.

As they walked down the stairs to the basement, he was hit with the smell of the boxes in the squad room, only much stronger. There were two large industrial fans aimed at one corner of the room where the fire had been. He could see from the scorch marks where the accelerant had been and the damp musty odor made it clear that the sprinklers had limited the fire to this one location. He made his way around, looking for any footprints or other signs of the person who had set the fire, but found none. There were six windows high up on the walls, but none seemed to have been tampered with.

Jennifer saw him examining the windows and asked, "Do you have any idea how whoever set this got into the basement?"

"I'm sorry to admit that the front and side doors were unlocked. We have always had a policy of being open to anyone. We may need to reexamine that after this. Anybody could have walked in and set the fire. Obviously, it appears to be someone interested in the records from the orphanage, but whom or why I have no idea. Ah, here's Sister Evangeline now."

Sister Evangeline appeared to be upwards of eighty years old. She had a heavily wrinkled face and was slightly bent over, possibly from osteoporosis. Her smile, however, was completely captivating and her eyes bright as candles set deep within their holders. "I've been waiting for someone to ask me about it," she said before hitting the final step.

"About what?" Jennifer asked.

"Father Martin's brother," she answered.

"What, me?" Michael asked.

"No. The other one."

Both Jennifer's and Michael's mouths literally fell open.

"Maybe we should take this upstairs where we can explore this in more comfortable surroundings," Sister Mary Francis said, looking as shocked as the two detectives.

Chapter 36

Sister Mary Francis led everyone into the library. One of the sisters was at a table reading. Sister Mary Francis asked if it would be too much trouble for her to take her book elsewhere and to have Sister Mary Agnes bring them tea. The Sister immediately exited the room.

"Sister Evangeline, do you have something to tell us about the fire?" Michael asked.

"Well, maybe," she answered, "but I was thinking more about Anthony. I believe he was your brother as well detective. It could also involve the fire, but that would be conjecture."

"Maybe you could start from the beginning," suggested Jennifer, in a kind and respectful voice.

"Well, it all goes back to the orphanage. We were one of the few Catholic orphanages still around in the early '70's. The Roe v Wade case hadn't been passed yet and unwed teenage pregnancies were still a social disgrace to families back then. Schools would not let young women stay in school like today. It was a very different time for society. Young people were starting to hear about a sexual revolution, but society hadn't caught up. There were abortions, but they often had horrible consequences; terrible mutilations and deaths. Homes for unwed mothers were a common alternative and often the children were given up for adoption. When adoptions were not prearranged, orphanages served as an alternative. They thrived until the late '70's and early '80's until State regulations and financial burdens forced them out of business. That's what ultimately caused us to close our orphanage. It all seems so long ago. I was a novice when I was assigned to St. Anne's. I was young and strong and that's how I came to know Anthony."

"I'm sure it was wrong, but the sisters talked among themselves about how the children came to be there. We often read their records to confirm age and were privy to their histories. Your grandmother, Michael, may I call you Michael detective?"

"Of course Sister, Michael is fine."

"Well your grandmother, Margaret McGinnis, wanted Anthony to be placed in a Catholic orphanage. She gave him the name Anthony after Saint Anthony, the patron saint of lost things. It came to be an apt name. As no father was listed, it was up to the Mother Superior at the time to come up with a last name for the birth certificate. She chose DeMarko. He was born with a shock of chestnut brown hair, just like you and Fr. Martin, and he had a birthmark on his thigh that resembled an angel. Anthony was a difficult baby. He was given to colic. That made it difficult to place him as a newborn, a prime time for adoption."

"He was first placed in a foster home when he was about 15 months old. That turned out to be the first of many unfortunate placements over the years. He was with that family for a little over a year when they were charged with child endangerment, among other things. He was returned to us just before his third birthday. He was malnourished and had obvious signs of abuse. He was with us till he was about five and became very attached to the sisters. He seemed anxious to please them, but remained a little stand offish with the other children. He was big for his age and did not share well, causing some concern, but responded immediately to correction. It was blamed on his earlier abuse. He always seemed genuinely repentant and loving to the sisters. We nicknamed him Angel.

"When he was five he was placed again. This time the family was interviewed in-depth to make sure that they were sincere about wanting to ultimately adopt Angel. It was a solid Catholic home; in fact, parishioners. And we followed up personally, not trusting the state to determine conditions. Besides, Angel was enrolled in our school so we remained in contact. Everything was fine until Mrs. Whaley got pregnant. She had twins when Angel was about six and a half. The Whaleys were great about making sure that Angel didn't feel left out and he seemed to be adjusting until Mrs. Whaley got pregnant again. At first it seemed that Angel just withdrew a little from the family. He started getting into fights at school. Then he started to take it out on the twins; teasing them, hiding their toys, things like that. Finally he took to abusing the twins. Ultimately, he broke one of the twin's arms and had to be physically restrained to keep from doing more damage. He was returned again to the orphanage."

"Sister, you seem to be very familiar with Angel and his history. Are you this knowledgeable about many of the orphans you took care of?" Jennifer asked.

"And when did you put it together that he was my brother?" asked Michael.

As Sister Evangeline was about to answer, Sister Mary Agnes came into the room with the tea. As she was placing the tray on the table, Sister Evangeline said, "All in good time. But Sister Mary Agnes may know a bit about it. She is the one who scanned all the adoption and placement files onto a disk a few years back."

"You mean you have copies of all the files from the basement on disk?" asked Jennifer.

"Oh yes ma'am. They've been updated to Word. They're on file here in the library."

"Excuse me for a moment, ladies," said Michael as he pulled his phone out of his pocket. Walking away from the table, he dialed the squad room. "Higgins, get those file boxes out of the squad room. I don't care where. No, don't destroy them, yet just move them somewhere else, maybe the garage. I'll explain later. Yeah, thanks. The same to you."

As he was heading back to the table, Jennifer asked him how he took his tea with more than a hint of laughter in her voice. Michael sat down and put a spoonful of sugar and a little cream in his tea.

"We will need copies of those files, Sister."

"Just give me the ip address. I'll have them transferred," said Sister Mary Francis. Jennifer gave the address of the precinct server to her, saying thank you.

"Go on with your story, Evangeline," Sister Mary Francis said as Sister Mary Agnes left to transfer the files.

"To answer your question, Detective Palmer, different sister's seemed to attach themselves to different children. I really don't understand why. Perhaps it was the timing of my introduction to Angel. It was just before I took my final vows. Maybe it was my age. I'm not really sure but I found a connection that continued until I could no longer keep track of him. The connection to Father Martin occurred much later. At any rate, when Angel got back, we expected it would be a problem, but he seemed to pick up right where he was when he left. He couldn't do enough to please the sisters. At eight and a half he was tall and strong. He'd be there to bring the groceries in from the car. He excelled at school sports and made a few friends. He was a bit lazy in his homework but was smart as a whip. And he had grown up to be very good looking. In fact, that's how I knew he was your brother, Michael. Well not yours exactly, but Fr. Martin's. Angel was long gone before Father Martin got here, but as soon as I saw him, I recognized him. At first I thought it might be Angel, but he was much too young. I also had seen pictures of you, Michael, in the papers. The family resemblance was uncanny. Gradually, I found out that your mother's name was Mary and that your Grandmother was Margaret McGinnis and that was that. I really couldn't tell anybody because adoption records are sealed; but I had no doubt that Angel was your brother."

"Well, what happened to Angel?" Michael asked.

"That's difficult to say. He appeared to be thriving with us here at the orphanage. He had just started high school in '84 when the orphanage shut down. He was placed in a foster home in East Liberty by the state. He came back to the convent a few times just to see me and a few of his old teachers. He was terribly unhappy. The last I saw him was after he had been arrested for robbing a liquor store on Penn Avenue. I went to the hearing. He was convicted and sent to Shuman Detention Center. For many years after that we would receive Christmas cards signed Angel, but they stopped about six years ago."

"Humm," said Michael. "I'm not sure that they did. They may have just changed form."

"What do you mean Michael?" asked Sister Evangeline.

"I'm not sure," said Michael.

Jennifer took the police sketch out of a folder she had placed on the table and showed it to Sister Evangeline. "Do you think this could be him?" she asked.

"There is no doubt in my mind," answered Sister Evangeline. "In fact, I thought I saw him around the church a few months ago, but when I looked back, he was gone."

"Do you happen to have any of those Christmas cards or envelopes?" asked Jennifer.

"Oh goodness; I might have a card, but I doubt I would have any of the envelopes. I did notice at the time that one was from France and another was from Italy. The others were all from Pittsburgh."

"God bless your memory, Sister," said Michael.

"Detective Michael, do you think Angel set that fire?" asked Sister Mary Francis.

"There's a distinct possibility that he's trying to hide his identity and his past, Sister," Michael answered.

Jennifer finished her tea and stood up. "Sister Evangeline, you've been a great help to us. Father Martin only found out last night that he had a brother. I think he would be happy to talk to you about it."

Michael reassured Sister Mary Francis that he didn't think they were in any future danger but it might be a good idea to keep the doors locked at night, at least for a while.

As they were leaving, Sister Mary Francis said to Michael, "Father Martin takes his tea the same way you do." She had a smile on her face.

Chapter 37

As they left the convent and headed for their car, Jennifer said, "I've always wondered what a convent was like. I pictured a cold stark place with crosses all over and stern faces, but that place is like a home. You can feel the warmth, the, I don't know, joy? I was completely comfortable."

"Funny thing about Catholics, they're like real live people," said Michael, with a laugh. "I better call Alan and let them know we have identification."

Michael pulled out his phone, dialed Alan's phone and put the call on speaker as he settled into the driver's seat. "Alan, it's Mike, we've got an ID on Angel. His name is Anthony DeMarko. He was raised at St. Anne's old orphanage. The DNA match is because...Where are you? It sounds like you're outside."

"Yeah," said Alan. "We thought we'd have lunch out and air out our clothes. Can't seem to get that smell out of them. Found a lunch truck outside the park down from the...Ugh!" The phone appeared to hit a hard surface, followed by frantic noises; screams and voices came over the speaker.

"Alan! Alan, what's going on?"

"Call an ambulance! Alan! Alan! Hold on." The voice appeared to be Jeff. "Ala... Oh my God; Aaugh." The phone went dead. About the same time, a call came over the car intercom, "Officer down, officer down. West North Avenue and Brighton Avenue, Allegheny Commons Park. All units respond."

"Put your belt on," said Michael, turning on the sirens and lights while starting the car.

"Why the hell would he shoot FBI agents?" Jennifer exclaimed.

"You're assuming its Angel," said Michael.

"Who the hell else would it be?" answered Jennifer.

"I don't know, but I intend to find out," said Michael racing down route 65 toward town.

It took about 15 minutes for Jennifer and Michael to reach the scene. There were officers everywhere. The area had been roped off with 'Police Line, Do Not Cross' tape. Michael found the first place available to park the car and he and Jennifer sprinted to the center of the large group of people standing in a cluster about ten feet off North Avenue. An ambulance had pulled onto the grass and two attendants were about to lift a gurney into the back. Michael flashed his badge and put his hand up for them to stop. Jeff Hooper was covered with a sheet and strapped down on the gurney. He was in obvious pain, but conscious. There was blood seeping through the sheet and dripping down his left arm. "Jeff, what happen?" Michael panted out.

"Alan's dead! I've been hit. It had to be Tony. Had to be. Never made a sound."

"Tony?" Michael asked. But before Jeff could answer, the paramedics interrupted.

"We need to get him to the Hospital."

"Where are you taking him?" Michael asked.

"Allegheny General; you can talk to him there if he makes it. We have to go," said the paramedic shutting the door.

Deputy Chief Morrow approached the ambulance. "It was a sniper. The shots came from a stairwell in the apartment building across the street," he said, pointing to a white brick building on the other side of North Avenue. We found two shells on the fourth floor landing; same M.O. as O'Shaughnessy. Witness saw a man with a suitcase leaving the building from a side entrance. He had a shaved head and was clean-shaven."

"He changed his appearance, but how did he know they would be here?" said Michael.

"Maybe he followed them here," said Morrow.

"And had time to find a building and climb 4 floors with a rifle, and time to aim a shot? Nah. He had to know they were coming here."

While Michael had been talking to Jeff, Jennifer was further into the crowd where the coroner was zipping up a black bag with Alan's body inside. She came back and joined Michael. "One shot. Entered through the right eye. Death was instantaneous."

Michael looked at Jennifer. "Jeff called him Tony. Was there enough time for him to hear me tell Alan the name? Bob, did anyone find Alan's phone?"

"Yeah, it was picked up and marked. Why?"

"I want to know if it was on speaker," answered Michael.

"Well I can get it for you, but I doubt it will help. It had been stepped on; apparently by Hooper trying to get to Alan. Shall I have it brought over?"

"No, but I want it to be examined for recent calls and tracked for location in the last three days. If you can have it done before the FBI gets hold of it."

Jennifer instantly understood, but obviously Morrow didn't. "Before the FBI gets to it? Why? What difference would that make?" asked Morrow.

"Just a hunch. Can you do it?"

"Well sure. What are you expecting to find?"

"I'm not ready to say yet. You know how the agency always seems to complicate things. Send a copy of the report to Jen's laptop when you get it."

"OK. I'll get on it."

Michael and Jennifer stuck around for about another ten or fifteen minutes and then headed to the hospital.

Chapter 38

As Michael and Jennifer settled back into the car, Michael turned off the lights and siren and started the car, but he did not move it right away. The hospital was only about seven blocks up on the same street. Michael knew they would be prepping Jeff for a while before they would have any hope of talking to him.

"Jennifer, when they were questioning Martin, did they seem to already know he was not the perpetrator?"

"Now that you mention it, they did seem to go pretty soft on him. I just chalked it up to his being a priest and his lawyer being intimidating, not to mention your brother. Why do you ask?"

"I think they knew he wasn't a suspect. I think they knew who Angel was all along." He started to pull out of the mass of vehicles and eased his way past the now dispersing cars.

"Michael, you make it sound like some kind of conspiracy. This is the FBI. Why would they be keeping information from us?"

"You've obviously never worked with spooks before. They hold their cards close to their vest. They never share more than they have to. Jeff called the shooter Tony. And how did Angel know where they would be? I think they had set up a meeting and something went wrong."

"Why would they do something like that?"

"That's what I hope to find out," said Michael pulling up to the curb just outside of the emergency room. Jennifer pulled a Police sign out of the glove box and put it on the dash as she and Michael exited the car.

Once inside, it was exactly as Michael expected; highly organized confusion. Nurses headed in all directions, doctors being paged over the loudspeakers, along with regular beeps.

Michael showed his badge to the receptionist and asked where they had taken the shooting patient. She motioned down hallway 'C' and started to say something that Michael didn't wait to hear. There were two doors at the start of Hall 'C' and about half way down the hall was a large nurse's station. Just past the station the hall opened to a series of curtained bays. All of the activity appeared to be centered on the middle bay. Michael stopped at the nurse's station and again showed his badge. In a rare stroke of luck, Michael recognized the head nurse. She had attended to him a year ago when he took a bullet in his thigh. "Monica, good to see you. Wish it were under better circumstances."

"Well, Detective Davis. What brings you back?"

"The guy in the bed over there," Michael answered. "This is my partner, Detective Palmer."

"Well, I certainly hope he's a better partner than patient Detective," Monica responded.

"Monica, how does it look for agent Hooper? Any possibility I can talk to him?"

"You know better than that Mike," she replied. "I'll get the doctor for you. It's Dr. Garrett; the same doctor who treated your leg. It's his call."

As she went to get the doctor, Jennifer said, "she seems to have your number."

"Oh, that's just her Nurse Ratched persona. She's a sweetheart once you get to know her."

Monica came back with Dr. Garrett. "John so good to see you," said Michael. What can you tell me about Agent Hooper? Any chance I can talk to him?"

"Mike, he's in real bad shape. The bullet nicked his heart and is lodged in his lung. He lost a lot of blood. We've medicated him and stopped the bleeding, but the wall of the left aortic chamber could perforate at any time. He's conscious, but barely. Is it absolutely necessary for you to talk to him?"

"How likely is it that I can talk to him later?"

"Not giving any odds on this one. It's an extremely delicate and lengthy procedure."

"Then I guess it's very important."

"I know you won't like it, but I'll have to observe and if I say stop, you need to stop. Do I have your word?"

"Yes Doc. If I had a choice I wouldn't ask."

"OK, but make it quick."

Michael, Jennifer and Dr. Garrett entered the bay. Jeff was attached to an IV with a second tube inserted directly into his lung, pumping air in and keeping his lung from collapsing; there were numerous monitors stuck to his upper body, but he seemed alert. He gave an extremely grim smile upon seeing Michael and Jen.

"Jennifer, will you marry me?" he said with a slight laugh that brought on a coughing spell. You could hear the phlegm railing in his throat.

"If you promise to get through this, I'll think about it," Jennifer answered.

"Jeff I've got to ask a few questions. You knew Angel's identity, didn't you?"

"Yes. And he changed his name. It's Anthony Wallace now, but there are others that he uses."

"Were you and Alan planning to meet with him?"

"Yes. He was what we call an asset. We were sent to extricate him if we could, and disable him if we couldn't."

"Disable?" Jennifer asked.

"Terminate," Jeff answered. "He'd gone rogue; independent, if you will. We were assigned to reel him in. He obviously didn't plan on cooperating."

"How did you plan to bring him in?"

"We were prepared to transfer a hefty sum into an account he used. The number is on a slip of paper in a compartment of Alan's wallet." His speech was becoming more and more labored.

"Jeff," Michael said softly, "Why are you admitting all this? The agency will be furious that you talked to us," Michael asked. "I expected to have to pry this out of you."

"Michael, I don't expect to make it. Even if I do, I'm of no more use to the agency. You don't retire from the division I'm in. I'm dead either way. You're one of the few good guys left, Michael. I know he's your brother, but you have to get him." Jeff had another coughing spell, leading Dr. Garrett, who had been watching an electric display, to signal to Michael that it was time to stop.

"Jeff, if you get through this, we'll do what we can to help you."

Jennifer was watching Jeff's eyes start to roll up and he was blinking rapidly.

"Code Blue" shouted Dr. Garrett. "Out, now!" he said to Michael and Jennifer. As they were moving to leave, nurses came running in with a cart. Michael and Jennifer moved to the nurses' station and watched the flurry of activity. They heard the "Clear" twice in rapid succession.

After a minute or two, Dr. Garrett came out. "He's stable, barely. No more questions. We're taking him into O.R. now. I don't believe what I heard in there."

"Good. Don't believe it or even think about it. Consider it doctor-patient communication, John, and thank you," said Michael.

"Save him if you can doctor," added Jennifer. "In spite of what you may have heard in there, he's a good man."

Michael put his arm around Jennifer's shoulders and they exited Hall 'C'.

"I wish you'd been wrong," Jennifer said softly to Michael.

Chapter 39

Michael and Jennifer headed back to the precinct, but were stopped before they even got to the elevator. The desk sergeant called Michael over and told him to report to Deputy Chief Morrow immediately. He also told him the Police Commissioner and Mayor were waiting for them. They took the stairs up to the Second Floor rather than wait for the elevator and headed to the Deputy Chief's office. Marge, Morrow's secretary, directed them across the hall to the conference room. She also told them just to go in; they were expected.

The Commissioner was the first to see them entering. "Nothing's ever simple when you're involved, is it Davis?"

"Give them a chance to sit down, Steve," interrupted the Mayor. "How are you today, Detective Palmer?"

"You know Detective Palmer, Bill?" asked the Commissioner.

"I've had the pleasure."

"Our daughters share an interest in ballet," Jennifer said quickly.

"What's up?" asked Michael, adding almost immediately "We had a chance to interview Hooper at the hospital. He's nip and tuck; in surgery as we speak."

"Michael, what was the urgency about breaking down the phone? Did you know something?" Asked Morrow.

"Just a suspicion," said Michael. "The shooter, I'm relatively certain was Angel, had to know where they were going to be. Also, they didn't mention anything about their excursion yesterday. We'll need to get the itinerary from yesterday and I need to see Whitfield's wallet."

"Slow down. We already got their itinerary and we broke down Whitfield's phone and are picking Hooper's up as we speak. What do you expect to find in Whitfield's wallet?" Morrow asked.

"I believe we will find an off-shore account number in it," Michael answered.

Deputy Chief Morrow pushed a button on a phone sitting on the conference table. "Have Whitfield's wallet sent in as soon as possible. It should be in the property room. Thanks." Turning to Chief Schubert, Morrow asked "How much can we share with Detectives Davis and Palmer?"

"Might as well let them in on everything. They seem to be ahead of us anyway," answered Schubert.

"Michael, it appears that Whitfield and Hooper were not connected with the FBI. When we notified them of the murder, they didn't know what we were talking about. CJIS had no record of a DNA match on the sample we sent, only familiars, and CODIS doesn't release them. The NCIC, however, will and that is where the list we have been using came from. The FBI had no record of a match in their files. Of more interest, Whitfield and Hooper did not go to investigate those matches in the Harrisburg area. They went to Langley. FBI's main office is in D.C. and CJIS is in Clarksburg, West Virginia. The main office of the CIA is at Langley. They deny any knowledge of Whitfield or Hooper or any meetings yesterday. Steve, I mean Chief Schubert, called in a favor and was able to confirm, however, that a meeting did take place yesterday. Details were not available. The local FBI are now involved and attempting to identify our friends. Also, a copy of the DNA report was sent to the CIA the day before Whitfield and Hooper arrived. That was the same day I received confirmation of their assignment to the case. Your tip about the phone proved spot on. Whitfield made a call to a burner about 10 am yesterday. The call was received in the general vicinity of St. Anne's."

"Well, we can add a few more details," said Michael. "Angel's full name is Anthony DeMarko, alias Tony Wallace. He was a contract killer, or asset, according to Jeff. At least some of his work was independent, but he was used by 'the agency' as Jeff put it. Whitfield's and Hooper's assignment was to bring him in, with the help of a bribe, or terminate if he was non-compliant. Jeff assumed he'd chosen non-compliant." Michael paused for a minute and appeared to be deciding how to phrase something. "Angel is also a brother I never knew I had. He spent most of his youth in an orphanage connected to St. Anne's, interrupted twice by short spans in foster homes and, at least on one occasion, incarceration at Shuman Center. There should be a record of his arrest around 1984, give or take a year. His experiences were less than ideal."

Chief Schubert, who had been standing, fell back into a chair, his mouth wide open. The Mayor, with a noticeable grin on his face said, "Just a tad ahead of us; wouldn't you say Steve?"

"Damned nice job, Davis," Deputy Chief Morrow said. "Do you know where he is, too?"

"No. Not yet anyway," Michael said.

"Another thing," Jennifer said. "I recorded Jeff's statements, but we can't use them for any legal purposes. I did not inform him that he was being recorded. I can send a copy to you."

"Better to transcribe and leave a paper copy for Deputy Chief Morrow. I would prefer it not go through the network," said Schubert. "I doubt any of this will ever see the light of day. Oh, and change any written identification of Whitfield and Hooper to 'government agents' without any attribution to a specific agency. Do you have a problem with that, Bill?" Schubert asked the Mayor.

"Under the circumstances, none at all."

"Mike, by rights I should remove you from the case now that we know of your relation to this Angel character...," Morrow said, but was cut off by Chief Schubert. "The hell you will. I think we're better off waiving policy on this one. They are too involved to replace them now and they clearly work best together. No, let the detective maintain the lead." Turning to Michael, he added, "I trust you'll keep us up to date and call in help as you need it, Mike?"

"Of course, Chief," Michael answered.

"You should know that Dr. Garrett was present during the interview. It was a medical necessity," said Jennifer.

"Dr. John Garrett is an old acquaintance. I advised him to keep anything he overheard as doctor – client privilege. I don't think we have a problem," Michael added.

"I guess we'll have to trust him," said Chief Schubert.

"Is there anything else gentlemen?" asked Michael.

"No. I think that's enough for right now," said Morrow. "And Jennifer, I assume you'll be writing up your reports. Use special care and keep it as vague, but accurate, as possible."

The Mayor stood up and asked Jennifer, "Will I be seeing you both at the concert? Do you need any more tickets?"

"Well, Meagan and I are confirmed, but Michael's not sure about protocol; fraternization and appearances and all," Jennifer said.

"Oh, bull shit on that. You really should attend Mike," the Mayor said.

Chief Schubert and Deputy Chief Morrow looked stunned.

"It's a public event. I see no problem."

"Well, I guess now I'll have to," said Michael. "You've just made Meagan very happy."

"Consider it a reward for a job well done," said the Mayor adding, "I'm running late for a council meeting. Keep me informed. I have a feeling I'll be explaining all this to the Governor. Make me look good gentlemen," he said and then, looking at Jennifer, "and lady." And with that he was gone.

"Well, it appears the inmates are running the asylum. Keep me informed, Bob. Nice job detectives," said Chief Schubert. And he exited also.

"I guess I'm not the only one who likes cliques," Chief Morrow said, shaking his head as he went across the hall to his office.

Now alone in the conference room Jennifer looked at Michael and they both broke into laughter.

Chapter 40

They were still composing themselves when Chief Morrow came back into the room with Alan's wallet and a piece of paper in his hands. He tossed the wallet to Michael. "It's already been dusted for prints and the contents logged. There were no signs of any paper with numbers. I also had a driver's license for Anthony Wallace pulled. Here's the current address and the picture on file. There are three vehicles registered to him; a 2014 white Chevy Malibu, a 2015 red Ford 150 pickup, and a 1998 Harley Davidson cycle. All the details have been sent to both the county and state police with an APB. The transit police are loading the data into facial recognition as well as sending a delay and notify bulletin."

Michael was listening as he emptied the wallet. "You may want to add armed and dangerous," as he turned the wallet inside out. Sure enough, there was a small slice in the lining of the outer cover. Michael ripped the lining and pulled out a slip of paper with an international phone number and below it a 16 digit account number on it.

Michael handed the slip of paper to Morrow. "Bob, can you see if you can track down this institution? I'd probably avoid the CIA, if possible. Oh, and let the Bishop know. I have a feeling it's related to a mysterious donor they have been trying to track down."

"Have you been moonlighting, Davis?"

"It ties into St. Anne's."

Jennifer interrupted him. "Michael, did you look at the address on the driver's license? It's the site of the old orphanage next to the Mother House."

Michael looked at the driver's license information and picture. It was somewhat difficult to ignore the picture of what he now knew for sure was his brother and concentrate on the address. "Bob, can you get the swat team on this?"

"Have to be County. It's out of our jurisdiction."

"The county, then. If you can, have them wait for us to get there."

"Michael, I'll do what I can, but once they're in, it's going to be their show," Morrow said.

"That's fine. I doubt they'll catch him there but it might tell us what vehicle to look for."

"I have to get back to the Feds. Any idea what to tell them?"

"I wouldn't worry about the FBI, but try to stall any information from getting to the CIA. I have a suspicion they're in this up to their eyeballs and looking for a certain outcome. Beside's, you'll probably need them to track down the off-shore account."

"In spite of what the Commissioner says, you're personally involved in this. Watch your back, Mike. If you're right about the spooks, they'll be looking for a scapegoat."

"We'll be careful, Chief," added Jennifer, putting her laptop back in her shoulder bag and heading for the door. "If the witness was right, he's shaved his head and beard. Make sure the APB lists that. They'll probably catch Martin!"

Michael already had Martin on his cell as they exited the door.

Chapter 41

"Hey Mickey, how's the case going?"

"No time for that Marty," Michael said, going down the stairs and heading for the car. "Is Joanna still with you?"

"Yeah, we're down on the River Walk. She hasn't been here since the Three Rivers Stadium days. Going to be headed to the airport soon."

"You might want to put a hold on that," Michael said, flipping Jennifer the keys. "You'll probably be picked up by the police. There's an APB out on Angel. Joanna might have to take another flight."

"I'm sure I can explain everything to them. I just need to pull up to drop off."

"Marty, the APB says armed and dangerous. You could be shot by some nervous badge before you get that chance. I suggest you get over to my place and hunker down until you hear from me. There's a spare key under the flower pot on the porch. There's plenty of food. As soon as I can get free, I'll get Joanna to the airport, but right now I have to get to St. Anne's and I still need to warn Sister Mary Francis. A SWAT team is headed to the house next to the convent. She needs to get the sisters out of danger."

"What the hell?" Martin replied.

"I'll explain later. Oh, and I wouldn't count on seeing any more mystery checks anymore."

"Well, aren't you just full of good news! We'll get to your place and I'll call a cab for Joanna."

Michael heard Joanna over the speaker, "The hell you will. I want to see this through. I'll keep him safe, Michael. Go do your job."

"Thanks Jo," said Michael and hung up. He was about to find the number for the convent before he realized that Jennifer was already explaining the situation to Sister Mary Francis.

"Thank you, Sister. I'm sure you'll be safe, but please take all precautions. As soon as you can, lock down the school. I'll call the local police and let them know you're in the middle of dismissal. Keep things as calm as you can."

Michael had caught the gist of the conversation and understood exactly what was happening. He was on the car phone with Morrow. "Yes, the school is directly behind the property and dismissal is already going on. Get them to hold back. If he is in the house, we don't want to take a chance of making him move. No, the kids are already outside, lined up for the buses. Any changes could cause panic. The walkers are already released. We need to get the kids out of there."

Jennifer looked seriously worried. "Michael, they're just a little bit younger than Meagan. You don't think he'd hurt a child, do you?"

Michael could hear the fear creeping into her voice. "No, Jen, I don't. He sends money to the church; he feels the sisters are his family. He even went to that school. I can't see him hurting anyone there," he swallowed hard and continued, "unless he has to."

"Thanks a lot."

"This is not a time for lies, Jen," Michael said with as much comfort as he could put in to line.

Jennifer refocused, "Thank you Michael. I needed that."

"Pull up in front of the convent. It's out of the sight lines."

As they approached the church complex, Michael noticed the lineup of vehicles on the block just in front of the church. He was stopped by the road block that had been set up. He flashed his badge and was allowed to pass.

As they pulled up to the curb in front of the convent, he also saw another group of cars on the far side of the rectory. Obviously Chief Morrow had gotten through. He could see the front of the school from where they were parked. The children were getting on their buses, pushing and shoving; generally acting normally. Sister Mary Francis had managed to keep things as normal as possible.

All of the surrounding streets had been blocked off. A few cars were let in to the pickup area to get their children. There were two female officers dressed as crossing guards directing traffic. They were told there was a fire a block over and ushered the traffic in and out of the area. To all appearances, things were normal for a Friday afternoon.

Sister Mary Francis had called Michael from a phone in the school office. During the school day the phones were forwarded to the school. Michael and Jennifer were just leaving the car and taking up a position beside the convent. The location was identified on Michael's phone as the school office. As soon as she had hung up from talking to Michael, Sister Mary Francis had called over to the convent to have the few remaining sisters come over to the school under the guise of helping with the dismissal of the students. She cautioned them to walk casually as if it was a normal activity. Sister Evangeline was staying behind to lock up the convent.

As the sisters crossed the parking lot to the school, no one noticed the figure of an old priest crossing from the area of the house. He was wearing glasses and dressed in the usual black cassock with a biretta, the three cornered cap with a small pom-pom, on his head. He walked gingerly with a cane for assistance and seemed to be reading from a small book held in his right hand. As the last of the sisters entered the school, he entered the backdoor of the convent. The smell of smoke still hung in the air from the previous night's fire.

It took about 45 minutes to clear the school. There were a few stragglers who were gathered in the school office. Sister Mary

Francis called the number that she was given by the Beaver County Police and reported that dismissal was basically over.

Michael and Jennifer had been waiting beside the convent. When they saw the SWAT team moving in, they headed up toward the house to report to the commander in charge.

In what seemed like a matter of seconds, the house was surrounded by police officers in full gear. Michael and Jennifer were approaching the command center in front of the house. Heavily armored vehicles were covering the house from the front of the structure and more from the school parking lot. A loud speaker broke the silence that had settled in. "Anthony Wallace, if you're in the building, come out with your hands above your head." After about a minute, the notice was repeated and this time, "We have the house surrounded." Again, no response.

A phalanx of police from the SWAT team moved toward the front door of the house. There was no visible movement from inside. One of the vehicles in front of the house reported that there were no heat traces from inside the building. Three officers approached the front door. One officer placed a tool under the front door and another worked a small cable with a camera on the end through the opening. He maneuvered the camera in a number of directions and nothing out of the ordinary was observed. An officer tried the door and, finding it locked, signaled to a forth officer coming up the walk with a hand-held battering ram. By now, Michael and Jennifer were about half-way between the house and the convent.

A signal was given by the lieutenant in charge to break in the door. Simultaneous with the blow came an explosion causing the entire doorway to fly as shrapnel in all directions. The windows on every side of the house shattered, sending glass shards in all directions. A cacophony of shouts, mixed with smoke and debris, streamed out of the scene, moving out from the center as police officers pulled back, protecting themselves as best they could. Michael and Jennifer were knocked to the ground by the strength of the blast. A shard of glass had whistled past

Jennifer's ear as she fell backwards on the lawn. Michael had caught another in his forearm. He pulled it out as he stood up and viewed the destruction. The officers who had been on the porch were being pulled back to safety as others approached on the run, entering the house through the gaping hole that the explosion had left. Within a minute, about twenty officers were inside the house, securing the site. A fire truck had pulled up onto the lawn, but there did not appear to be any fire.

After checking on Jennifer, Michael ran over to the lieutenant and briefly introduced himself. He asked if he could enter. "It's your life," the lieutenant answered. "It appears to be empty, but I can't speak to the structure or other booby traps." A paramedic approached, but Michael brushed him off. "It's only a scratch."

Michael and Jennifer cautiously entered the house. In an alcove off of the kitchen was a police scanner, still working and reporting the conversations franticly going on between the SWAT team and county police headquarters. "Location breached. Damn place wired. Collateral damage unknown. Five officers down. Status unknown." The chatter continued.

"He knew we were coming before we even got here," Michael said to Jennifer.

"What do you expect? He is your brother."

"Yeah, well, let's see if we can get to the garage. Maybe we can find out what he's driving."

"Ok" said Jennifer "but if we have time later, I'd like to look around. You can tell a lot about a person from their home."

"Obviously nothing he wouldn't blow up," said Michael.

They opened a door on the side of the kitchen and looked into the garage. There was a complete shop along the back wall. "You appear to take after him," Jennifer said looking at the shop.

"That's a metal shop," Michael said. "Explains the custom rifling on the guns and the explosives on the entry way. Probably made the silencers he uses here as well," Michael said, as he picked up a piece of pipe in the doorway.

Michael noticed that all three vehicles were still in the garage. He was not surprised. "He's got our moves all figured out," Michael said to Jen.

"Like I said, he's your brother" Jennifer replied.

"As." Michael said. "As I said."

"Thank you professor," Jen retorted. "So where is he now?"

Michael was about to answer when his cell phone rang. He looked at the caller I.D. It was Sister Mary Francis. "Yes Sister? No, we didn't catch him. Yes, a couple of injuries but there do not appear to be any fatalities. What's that? Sister Evangeline? Yes. Yes, I understand. Officer Palmer and I are on our way."

Jennifer looked at him. "In the convent?" she mouthed without speaking. Michael shook his head yes.

When he hung up, Jennifer said, "should we tell the lieutenant?"

"Look at this circus. Do you think we should put the sisters in the line of fire?"

"Let's go then. Nonchalant, Michael."

As they passed through the living room, Michael said to the lieutenant, "Going to check on the Sisters at the school and then the convent. See if they noticed anything as you were deploying."

The lieutenant waved him on, seeming to be glad to get any locals out of his hair.

Chapter 42

Sister Evangeline had gone to the library to watch the good sisters cross over to the school. When she saw that they were all safely inside, she passed through the office into the reception area. Looking out the window, she could see the SWAT team starting to arrive just beyond the rectory. She particularly noticed a few armored and camouflaged vehicles pulled abreast of the cars. "What has happened to this country that we have military vehicles on our town streets?" she thought. Shaking her head as she went, she crossed to the front door and secured the deadbolt and lock. She then turned and went down the center hall to the back door.

Sister Evangeline still wore the full habit of the Dominican Order of Sisters. Her black robe swept the floor as she walked, giving her the impression of floating. She was bent over from osteoporosis and arthritis and tended to hold her hands folded in front of her. Most of her fellow sisters had either given up the habit for street clothes or the shorter version of the habit. So many changes she had seen in her years.

She entered the kitchen and looked out the back window. The children were still getting on the buses. Everything looked normal to her but she locked the back door as she had the front and decided to go to the small chapel just off the reception area to say a prayer for the children's young souls. She floated slowly down the hall again and entered the chapel. Almost immediately, she saw the figure standing beside the window to her left. As he turned to face her, she felt the instant joy of recognition.

"Sister Evangeline. You have aged so," said the figure.

"Anthony! So good to see you." Her voice dropped off as she spotted the pistol in his hand. She knew little of firearms but she had seen enough TV to recognize that it had a silencer on the end of it. As she looked up toward his face, she also noticed a rifle slung over his shoulder. "Oh Anthony, tell me it's not true. You were always such a good boy."

"Was would be the operative word there Sister," Anthony answered. "The world has a way of bringing out our true talents." He paused and added, "I don't want to hurt you Sister, but we're in survival mode here."

"Anthony, is it true you shot Father Costello? And those two women?"

"I didn't have any choice, Sister. I was trying to confess. He just wouldn't let me. He was going to turn me in. And that young girl, she was evil. She took my gun. I couldn't help it. I tried to keep to evil people who deserved to die. I really did. It just got away. I had to, don't you see that? I had to."

"Anthony, your family is here. Your brothers are here. Did you know you had a sister? They are here for you."

"I've known about them for a while now, except a sister. How could anyone not see that Father Martin and I were related? And that detective, Michael, I'd kind of run into him years ago. I thought he was a banger then, but I followed the press. I realized who he was, too. But they can't help me. Don't you see? We're a triangle just like God; three people in one. Three different sides. It's too late for the reunion thing. Too many bodies, too many souls. No, I'm alone as ever, Sister."

Sister Evangeline had been moving closer and closer as they spoke. "Give me the gun, Anthony. Look outside. There's an army out there waiting to capture you. We can go out and explain it to them."

"Back up Sister" commanded Angel. "I don't want to kill you, but I will. Further back! Take a seat in that pew." A knock on the door distracted them both. "See who that is," commanded Angel, his voice unrecognizably cold and distant. "And no funny work or you'll be meeting God sooner than expected."

Chapter 43

"You heard what Michael said," Joanna said to Martin.

"It's my parish, Jo. I can't just sit at Michael's pretending nothing's happening," Martin replied. "Besides, I can have Grace run you to the airport if you change your mind."

They got back into the car and Martin took Route. 19 to Rochester Road to avoid the possibility of running into the police.

"How could our brother wind up as a contract killer?" asked Joanna.

"Lizzy Borden took an axe and gave her father forty whacks," answered Martin.

"I'm serious, Marty," said Joanna.

"One cannot predict human behavior," Martin replied in his best ministerial voice. "A child abandoned at birth; unfortunately placed in dysfunctional homes in his early youth; the only home he really ever knew shut down, leaving him on his own. His chances were 50/50 at best."

"Why does God allow such things to happen, Marty?"

"It is not for us to question the ways of the Lord, Jo. We were created with free will. If all the trials we face in life were controlled by God, there would be no reason for our existence. It is up to us to earn our place in heaven. What happened to Anthony was the work of man, not God. It appears you have worked out your demons. It is up to Angel to work out his. I hate to use such a trite cliché, but God works in mysterious ways. St. Thomas Aquinas in his 'Confessions'..."

"Yeah, yeah, I know the boiler plate, but he's our brother! It seems to me that God could have given him a break. When you get a chance, put in a word for him. Maybe you have an inside line," Joanna said with a touch of sarcasm in her voice.

"Sorry, I don't mean to preach. I don't really understand it any better than you. I was just trying to say that it was more environmental than genetic. He obviously was keeping track of the parish. I just wish he had introduced himself to me; given me a chance to let him know his family."

"For all you know Marty, you may have even heard his confession."

Joanna could tell from his face that the thought of that had not crossed his mind. Martin was visibly shaken by the thought. He was obviously running through the thousands of confessions he had heard, trying to recall one that might have been Angel's.

"Don't do that to yourself, Marty. I'm sorry I brought the subject up. You would have responded correctly if it had ever happened. We can't change the past. I've often wondered what my life would be if I hadn't gotten myself pregnant at 17, but then I look at my boys and realize how blessed I am."

They rode in silence for a while until Joanna asked, "what do you think about Michael and Jennifer? Michael would hate me for saying it but they are so cute together."

"One can only hope. They seem to be made for each other, but they're fighting it. I think it's a departmental thing that's keeping them from jumping in bed."

"Martin! How surprising coming from you."

"A collar doesn't keep you from being a male, sis," Martin said with a chuckle. "You have eyes. I think it's inevitable. Did you see how he is with Meagan? They already function better than many marriages I see. I just hope they can work it out. I'm sure that there are a lot of complications career-wise. I can't see Michael leaving the force."

"Jennifer also had problems with her first husband."

"What problems? Are you keeping secrets again?" Martin asked.

"Obviously not very well," Joanna responded. "It's just a conversation she and I had last night. Apparently, Jim was not very attentive to her needs." She saw the look on Martin's face. "Not in that way, Marty. I'm surprised. You have a dirty mind; a bit jaded, I guess. It's just that she felt alone, abandoned in a way. She was planning to leave him. Of course, that was before he was murdered. She was drawn into the police force because of their kindness after his death. I hope her feelings about Michael are not some form of gratitude."

"Even if that was true at some point, I think it has gone past that," replied Martin.

"Michael would have a fit if he knew we were discussing his life like this," Joanna said and they both started laughing.

"Well, let's not tell him. We're here." Martin parked the car a block in front of the church. "We can cut through a couple yards and hopefully make it to the convent. After we get in, I'll call Michael and let him know."

They made it to the convent without being noticed. They saw Michael's car parked in front of the convent. When they got to the front door, they found it locked. Martin knocked on the door.

Chapter 44

Angel looked out the side light of the front door. "Ah, one of my brothers and, if I had to guess, that's my sister with him. Let them in and no funny business, Sister." Sister Evangeline unlocked the front door and the pair rushed in.

"Thank you, Sister. I don't want to be mistaken for Angel..." Father Martin saw Angel and his pistol trained on Sister Evangeline.

"No, that wouldn't do at all," Angel said. "Close the door Sister," he added sternly. "Well, a family reunion. Can I assume you're my beloved sister?"

"Yes, Anthony, you assume correctly," said Joanna. My name is Joanna. Mother told me about you on her death bed. I promised to keep it a secret. The boys just learned about you last night. I'm sorry. I should have told them sooner. We should have looked for you. I was too caught up in my own life at the time. God, you look so much like Marty."

"Yeah, life sucks some times. I would have liked to meet dear old mom and da..."

A loud explosion interrupted their conversation. "I guess they decided to visit," said Angel with a forced laugh. "All of you into the chapel."

Sister Evangeline led the way. "Grab a seat," said Angel. "Is that your car out front?"

"No," Martin replied. "We parked a couple of blocks over. I didn't want to draw attention. They might have mistaken me for you."

Angel walked over to the side window and looked out on the chaos left by the explosion. "Can't take the chance of leaving now. Too much going on at the moment. Wish I had thought of a paramedics uniform."

"I see you've shaved your hair and beard," said Martin. "You might make it in the vestments. You could appear to be giving Extreme Unction. Go out in an ambulance with the wounded. I assume there are casualties?" said Martin.

"Oh, I doubt anyone was killed. I actually despise killing. Do you find that hard to believe, my dear brother? Just turned out to be a vocation. My marks all deserved to die. They were bad people. At least that's what my clients said."

"And what about the girl and her mother? What about Father Costello?"

"You're right about that Father. The girl probably deserved it, but her poor mother's only sins were of the flesh, but I couldn't take a chance. The girl had found my pistol. She tried to seduce me. She was a foul little bitch. Sorry, Sister, I didn't mean to offend you. And that damned priest; he wouldn't grant me absolution. He would have turned me in for sure. It's just a big mess." Angel had transformed into a penitent. His body language, his tone was totally different from the person barking out orders just minutes before. All of Joanna's instincts made her want to give him a hug; tell him it would be ok. As she stood up, a switch was flipped in Angel.

"Sit down!" Angel commanded. He took a roll of packing tape out of his pocket and told Sister Evangeline to bind his sibling's hands and feet. He watched carefully to make sure she was getting the binds tight enough. The he took the tape from her. "Sorry, Sister. It has to be this way," and he bound her hands. As he lifted her habit just enough to bind her ankles, he was shocked to see how frail her limbs were. Martin thought he saw a tear building in the corner of Angel's eye.

"Anthony, you don't want to do this. I can see how distressed you are. I can hel…"

"Shut up, damn it!" Angel said aiming the pistol at him. "Do I have to gag you, too?"

The three hostages were sitting together in one of the pews. Joanna was thinking of an article she saw on line that said you could break out of taped situations by violently spreading your wrists apart, tearing the tape. She looked at the strand of thread in the packing tape and doubted it would work. Even if it did, wouldn't the motion draw Angel's attention? No, best not to try it now.

Angel was pacing back and forth stopping to look out of the window now and then. After what seemed like an eternity, he watched as the fire trucks and the ambulance pulled away. There were teams of police going in and out of his home. The phone rang, startling all four of them.

"I should get that. It must be Sister Mary Francis, otherwise it would have transferred over to the school," said Sister Evangeline.

"Let it ring," replied Angel.

After the third ring, the phone went to message. "I'm sending most of the sisters back to the convent. Didn't want you to be worried by their return. Everything seems fine here. Just a few stragglers to be picked up. The police are starting a canvass of the neighborhood."

The message was on speaker, giving Angel an idea of what was going on. He thought he'd have to wait it out. He was trying to think of how to handle the additional sisters and decided to lock them up in the basement and made a mental note to make sure none of them had cell phones.

"How many of your sisters can I expect?" Angel asked Sister Evangeline.

"Well, I can hardly be sure. I don't know how many will be staying behind."

"I see you still have your wits about you, Sister. All right then, how many if they all came back, including Sister Mary Francis?"

"In total, 9, including myself."

"So, probably about 5 or 6. Not too bad. I should be able to handle that. Stand up Sister, time to greet your friends." After a brief pause while Sister Evangeline tried to stand up and maneuver out of the pew with her ankles tied, Angel said to Martin and Joanna, "Don't try anything. I've already shot one priest and fratricide won't prevent me from shooting another."

He pulled a knife out of his pocket. It was a switchblade, and flashed as it opened. Martin started to stand up, but Angel pivoted to aim his pistol past Sister Evangeline at Martin. "I wouldn't, Father," said Angel threateningly.

Martin sat back down and said, "We can still work this out Anthony."

"We'll see, we'll see," said Angel as he sliced the tape around Sister Evangeline's ankles. He motioned her to move down the hallway toward the kitchen. Angel followed Sister Evangeline down the hall.

"Stop here and turn to face the front," said Angel, sliding past her into the doorway of the library, out of sight of the kitchen. Within minutes, they heard someone try the backdoor only to find it locked. That was followed by a key turning in the lock and opening the door.

Chapter 45

Michael decided to check on Sister Mary Francis before heading to the convent. As Michael and Jennifer attempted to enter the school, two police officers in riot gear stopped them and asked for credentials. Normally they would just flash their badges and pass through police lines, but Michael was surprised to see that the officers insisted on holding the badges while they called into central control to verify their permission to enter. "Sorry sir. This one is a tight net. No mistakes" he said as he handed their badges back and stepped aside. "Quite understandable, thank you," replied Jennifer.

"Which way to the office?" asked Michael. The other officer pointed to his left. "About half way down this hall," he answered. Neither officer smiled.

"Serious business," Michael said to Jennifer. She just shrugged and led the way to the office. As they entered the doorway to the office, Michael noticed three children sitting along the wall, their feet dangling off the floor. Jennifer immediately walked up to them and said, "Your parents are on the way. They're being waved into the school yard right now. I'm Detective Palmer." She showed them her badge. They smiled back at her. "You've been very brave. I'm sure your parents will be excited to see you."

A nun walked up behind her and said, "Ok guys, gather up your things. We're going to go to the pickup area now. Come along." She gave Jennifer a wink and a smile. As they were leaving, Sister Mary Francis said to Jennifer, "You're very good around children. Do you have any of your own?"

"Just one. A girl who is in eighth grade."

Michael looked at Sister Mary Francis, "Well, now you know who your neighbor is."

"What was that explosion? Was anybody hurt?" asked Sister Mary Francis.

"The place was booby-trapped. A few members of the SWAT team were hurt, one pretty bad; they're all on their way to the hospital. Have the sisters headed back to the convent?" asked Michael.

"Not yet. They are helping to clean up the classrooms and make sure the place is ready for Monday. We only have one custodian. Keeps the price down. Parochial schools are dying, Michael. I'm sure Martin has complained to you about the difficulty of raising money."

"Well, I'm sorry to tell you, but it appears that in spite of all the horrible things he may have done, Angel was also your mysterious benefactor."

"Good heavens! You must be wrong."

"There are people running down the bank records now Sister, but, guilty or innocent, he appears to be the one. You know, nobody's all good or all bad. He is very attached to the parish."

"What a horrid day this is turning out to be," Sister Mary Francis said, cupping her forehead with her hand, elbow resting on the desk.

"Well, hopefully it's the end of it for you," said Jennifer sympathetically.

"If you think the sisters are done, call them together and Jennifer and I will escort them back to the convent," Michael said. "Maybe it's time for all of us to call it a day."

Sister Mary Francis picked up the microphone from the desk. "Attention Ladies. May I have your attention please? Finish up whatever you're working on and report to the front vestibule. You'll be escorted back to the convent together." She put the microphone down and said to Michael, "There are four police officers going through the building and two of our lay teachers still here. I'll be along as soon as they are all finished up. And Michael, take care of Martin. I'm rather hard on him at times but he's a good man. He works miracles of his own here. And don't you dare tell him I said that."

Michael smiled and said, "You're not too shabby yourself, Mother Superior." With that said, Michael left to wait for the group to amass in the vestibule.

"A second if I may, Jennifer?" said Sister Mary Francis.

Jennifer was already in the doorway, but stopped and turned toward Sister Mary Francis. "Yes, Sister?"

"And although I probably don't need to say it, take care of Michael. I can see from the chemistry between you that it's more than just a professional relationship."

Jennifer put her hand up and was starting to speak when the good Sister cut her off. "Even if you don't see it, others do. I wish you two the best."

Jennifer turned a bright shade of red and replied, "Thank you, Sister." And off she went to join Michael, slightly annoyed that everyone in Michael's and Martin's cadre of acquaintances could read right through her.

By the time she caught up to Michael he had everyone gathered together and was holding the door open. All together they numbered eight people. She and Michael walked behind, listening to the group laugh and jostle each other as they walked. Michael thought to himself, does devoting oneself to a higher power give them a sense of peace?

They got to the back door of the convent and found it locked. One of the sisters fished a set of keys out of her pocket and proceeded to open the door.

Chapter 46

As the entourage of sisters entered the kitchen, Michael held the screen door open. As the first sister entered the hallway she spotted Sister Evangeline standing still with her back to her and stopped, wondering what was wrong. The sister immediately behind her pulled up and glanced to the side. She spotted Angel standing in the doorway to the library with his pistol held at waist level pointed straight at her. A ripple moved through the line of nuns due to the abrupt stop.

The hairs on the back of Michael's neck stood on end as he sensed the tension passing through the line. He signaled to Jennifer to stay to the side. Reaching out, he silently withdrew the keys from the lock and handed them to Jennifer, motioning for her to step aside from the doorway. As he entered the doorway, he kept his head bowed forward, appearing to be distracted.

Angel had moved out of the doorway, motioning the sisters forward with the barrel of his pistol. He stepped into the hall just enough to see the kitchen doorway.

"That's right, Detective Davis. Come in further. Close and lock the door. Don't try to be a hero. Keep your hands where I can see them," Angel commanded in a hard, clear voice. "Where is your companion?"

"She will be coming along with Sister Mary Francis in a bit, Anthony" Michael answered.

"Funny how, all of a sudden, my dear siblings know my name," Angel shot back. "Now with your left hand use two fingers to remove your pistol from your holster and place it on the floor."

Michael was alarmed by the reference to siblings. How would Angel know that they knew his name, and why did he use siblings instead of brothers? In spite of his confusion, he did as he was told.

"Now pick up your pants legs. Any ankle holsters? Good. Kick the pistol over to me."

Michael kicked his 9mm Glock over toward Angel. Angel stepped the rest of the way into the hallway and looked at the sister closest to the pistol. "Pick it up and hand it to me."

The sister hesitated looking terrified. "I've never handled a gun," she said.

"Just pick it up by the handle and be careful not to touch the trigger. Glocks have hair triggers and no safety," said Angel. This threw the good sister into a full panic. "Oh, for Christ's sake, one of you pick it up and hand it to me." The sister standing next to the sister he had originally asked bent down and picked up the Glock. Angel could see from the way she flipped the handle into her palm that she was familiar with sidearms. "Don't even think about it, Sister. You don't have what it takes to kill a man. You'll hesitate and I'll drop you like a sack of potatoes." She glared defiantly at Angel, but handed him the pistol. "That's much better."

By now, Sister Evangeline had turned around and those closest to her could see the tape on her wrists. If any of them doubted the seriousness of the situation they were in, their thoughts were confirmed by the sound of his voice as Angel ordered them all back into the kitchen. As the six of them pushed in to the far corner of the kitchen, Sister Evangeline moved into the doorway of the kitchen.

"Not you, Sister" said Angel. "Stay where you are. Michael, stay where you are, too. The rest of you, empty your pockets. If I have to search you I will, but I need all cell phones on the counter."

Four of the sisters took phones out and placed them on the counter. Two of them were wearing a shorter contemporary form of the habit and Angel could see where the pockets were in their robes. One of the remaining sisters had a full habit on and Angel walked over to her and patted her down. The other sister was in street clothes and he could see that nothing resembling a phone was in her pockets.

"Ok. Now, into the basement."

"Why not let Sister Evangeline go with them?" said Michael. "You have me for a hostage."

"Oh, I have far more than you my dear brother," Angel answered with a laugh.

Michael wondered what Angel meant by his cryptic retort but knew from experience that it's best to keep a perpetrator engaged in conversation in a hostage situation.

"Anthony, it must have pained you greatly to have to shave your head. If you're anything like Martin or I, you're probably a bit vain about your locks."

Trying to stay focused, Angel ignored Michael. When he was sure that all of the sisters were in the basement he said, "Sister, throw the bolt on the basement door and wedge this chair under the knob." As soon as he was sure Sister Evangeline was following his orders, he turned to Michael. "No more than you had to lose your beard and ponytail after that undercover operation Michael, or should I call you Alex?"

Michael was visibly shaken by the fact that Angel knew about his earlier assignment.

"Oh yes brother, I recognized you at the time. I was actually surprised that my kin would be in such a rough gang. That was before I saw the results of your labor. I was actually proud of you for a while. Masterful job. I was already well established in my trade, but it didn't keep me from following your career. And when Martin was ordained and assigned to the very parish that had raised me, I was thrilled. I confess Joanna was a surprise. I didn't see that coming. I learned about her about the same time as you learned about me. How's that for timing?"

"And how did you learn about Joanna?" Michael asked, still trying to digest what he had just learned.

"Whitfield. He was one of my handlers in the Firm."

"But you killed him?" Michael asked, obviously trying to understand the whole picture.

"Before he could kill me," Angel responded. "By the way, how's Hooper doing? I always liked him. He had a real human quality. Shame he got in the way. Seems like that's the way things are going at the moment."

"When I left to come here, Jeff was in surgery. He was not expected to make it."

"A rare miss. Shame; quicker is always better."

"How did you get mixed up in all this, Angel?" asked Michael.

"Ah, there's a name I recognize better. Abandonment's a bitch, Michael. Doesn't matter why. Doesn't matter where. The good sister's did their best but it wasn't a mother and father. The ones they tried to find for me weren't any better. You're a rented child. A meal ticket. You learn to survive. But you must have a taste of that feeling, my dear brother. You were adopted by a family. You broke bread with them. You laughed, and, if I got good information, even loved, and you turned on them. See what I mean? You did your fucking job. Oh, you fucked them alright. Not like you fucked what was her name, Kathy, no? Close? Was it Kate? No you fucked them royal, right up the ass. They may have deserved it, but it's not the kind of thing you just walk away from, is it my brother? It bores in and eats away at you just like taking a life. You've tasted that one too, haven't you Michael? You think you're ready to handle ending another life Detective Davis?"

Sister Evangeline was standing by the basement door watching as Angel slowly stripped Michael bare, mentally. She could see the doubt, the shame draining the strength out of Michael.

She turned to Angel, "Stop it, Anthony. Just stop it." As the words were leaving her lips, she saw that Anthony was taking no pleasure in this. He was suffering along with his brother at the angst their paths had led them to; both riddled with guilt and regret for the acts they had committed. It was a big brother, broke and weary, explaining the fact of life to his younger brother.

Angel snapped out of it first; brought back to the issue at hand by Sister Evangeline's rebuff. "Snap to, Michael. I have another surprise for you in the chapel. Down the hall; Now! You too, Sister."

Chapter 47

Jennifer took the keys from Michael and silently slipped over to the edge of the library window. As she was doing so, she heard a man's voice addressing Michael. Taking a chance that his attention was fixed on Michael, she glanced in the window. She saw Angel straddling the doorway. When he moved into the kitchen, she quietly backed away from the back porch and headed back up to the school. The two remaining sisters were loading the last of the children into cars. She instructed one of them to bring the other to the office when they were finished. The two officers were still on guard at the doors and waved her past.

Jennifer headed straight for the office. Sister Mary Francis was gathering up her paperwork, getting ready to return to the convent. She looked up as Jen entered the door.

"What's wrong? You look frightened"

"You've a good eye Sister," Jennifer said. "Do you have an extra habit here?"

"No, but Sister Mary Margaret wears one. She's out putting the children in their cars. Why?"

"Angel has Michael and the other sisters held hostage in the convent. I have an idea, but I need a full habit to pull it off. I told the two sisters to report here when they were finished. I'll need her habit."

"I'll call the Lieutenant," said Sister Mary Francis.

"No! Not yet" said Jennifer. "I need time. I want you to wait till I'm changed and in the convent. Give me five minutes inside and then you can notify the SWAT team."

"I don't think I can do that. You'll be in danger."

"Angel is not very stable right now. Once SWAT moves in, someone's bound to be hurt. I think I have a better solution. I just need a little time."

Sister Mary Margaret and the other sister came into the office.

"Sister, I need you to switch clothes with me," said Jennifer, not waiting for Sister Mary Francis' answer.

"I don't think we're the same size," Sister Mary Margaret said, somewhat taken back.

"My clothes will be a little big on you, but I think it can work. It has to," said Jennifer already down to her slip.

"I certainly can't wear that," said Sister Mary Margaret, pointing to the pistol and holster Jennifer had placed on the desk.

"No problem. I'll be taking that with me," said Jennifer.

With some degree of discomfort, Sister Mary Margaret removed her habit and started to quickly put on Jennifer's clothes. The other sister and Sister Mary Francis were helping Jennifer adjust the borrowed habit. "I'm glad these aren't form fitting," Jennifer said. Sister Mary Francis tucked Jennifer's hair into the coif or headpiece and stepped back to view Jennifer.

"It's a little short," said Sister Mary Francis.

"It will have to do. Remember; give me five minutes inside before calling the Lieutenant," Jennifer said, picking up her pistol and tucking her hand under the habit.

Jennifer walked down the hall and nodded to the officers as she exited the school. They did not pick up on the exchange. She walked slowly down the path to the convent, tried the door and found it locked. She took out the keys that Michael had given her and, finding the right one, unlocked the door and walked into the kitchen, leaving the door unlocked.

Watching from her office, Sister Mary Francis watched Jennifer enter the convent and looked at her watch.

Chapter 48

Angel directed Sister Evangeline and Michael down the hall. He was careful to stay far enough behind to remove any temptation Michael might have to attempt to disarm him. When they reached the reception area, he motioned them into the chapel.

"Martin! Joanna! What the hell? I told you to stay away."

"Sorry Michael, it's my parish. I had to come."

"Well, well; it's a fucking family reunion," Angel said.

Angel had worked his way to the front window and stood to the side so he could glance out without turning his back. Michael rushed to his siblings. "If you hurt them, I'll kill you," Michael said.

"Don't worry, I'll make sure you're the first to go," answered Angel. He was taking quick glances outside the window. "That's your car out there, isn't that?"

"Yeah, but they have the streets cordoned off. You wouldn't make it a block."

"Maybe, maybe not. I've escaped tighter circumstances before."

"Yeah, I heard you're a real pro," Michael retorted as he slipped a pocket knife out of his pocket and dropped it into Martin's lap.

"Get away from them," ordered Angel.

Sister Evangeline saw Michael drop something into Father Martin's lap and spoke up to distract Angel. "Anthony, what did we do to make you like this? How could you choose this type of life?"

"Sister, you didn't do anything to cause this. My times here were the best of my childhood but that was a long time ago. I'm not a bad person. I just have an unusual profession. The people I extinguished were bad people. They were sinners. So were most of the people I worked for too, but it's a job. It's just the last few days things went wrong, all wrong. But I never forgot about you and the other sisters. I've been doing the best I could for you. I contributed to the church. I've been taking care of you."

"But Father Costello? The girl and her mother?" Sister Evangeline answered.

"I know, I know. That shouldn't have happened. I just couldn't let them expose me. I had to stop that. It just got out of control," Angel responded.

"So what are you going to do now?" asked Michael.

Angel didn't answer. He was watching as a few police officers worked across the street; talking to anyone who answered their doors, walking through yards. Finally, he turned away from the window and said to Michael, "You might as well sit down. We need to wait until they move further off down the street. You too, Sister."

Michael started to sit down next to Martin. "No, not there. Move down a pew," Angel said.

"If it's all the same to you, I'll stand."

"Suit yourself. Over there, against the wall then," said Angel. "Since we have some time, tell me about our parents; tell me what it was like living in a home with loving parents."

Joanna started to describe their lives growing up, hoping to take some of the tension out of the room.

It was while they were talking about their youth that Jennifer slipped into the kitchen. She saw the chair blocking the

213

basement door and slipped over and removed it. She undid the bolt. She opened the door and saw the sisters at the bottom of the stairs. She put a finger to her lips, directing them to stay quiet. She thought for a moment about closing the door and going to look for Angel, but decided it was best to get them away from the convent. She waved them up the stairs, gesturing with both hands to be as silent as possible. She saw the first sister look at the pistol in her right hand and put it back under her habit. As they emerged from the basement, she motioned them out the back door and pointed up to the school.

When the last sister was out the door, Jennifer closed it and, moving carefully, checked the hall. When she was sure it was clear, she moved into the library. From there, she opened the door into Sister Mary Francis's office and crossed the room, stopping at the door to the reception area. As cautiously as possible, she opened the door to the reception room just a crack. She could hear voices coming from the chapel.

Time was running out. Her five minutes was going to be up soon. She needed to think what to do.

In the chapel, Martin and Joanna were arguing about whom really let the dog out the day it was hit by a car when Angel said, "Stop!" He had noticed that two of the officers were coming across the street. He looked the other way and two more were crossing by the church. The muscles in Michael's body instinctively became tense.

Jennifer walked out the door from the office. "Sister Evangeline, where are the other...."

Angel pivoted and brought up his right hand with his 9mm automatic. Michael instantly recognized Jennifer's voice and broke for Angel. Angel reacted immediately, turning his attention to Michael and firing. The bullet hit Michael in his upper arm with enough force to knock him off his feet. As he was hitting the floor, he heard the second shot. Angel dropped to his knees and fell forward on the floor of the chapel. Michael looked out into the reception area and saw Jennifer dressed as a nun, with smoke coming from the hole in her habit.

In the confusion, Martin had managed to open the pen knife and cut his hands free. He turned and cut the tape from Joanna's hands, cut the tape from his legs and handed the knife to Joanna. He moved to his brother who was regaining his feet. Blood was running down his arm. Michael brushed him aside. "I'm fine. Get the gun from Angel."

Martin rolled Angel over. The gun was on the floor below his body. Martin kicked it away and took Angel's pulse from the vein in his neck. He was still breathing, but just barely. Martin looked down and saw that the bullet had hit him in the chest. Blood was gushing out of the cassock he was still wearing. "Joanna, find something and put pressure on the hole in his chest." Joanna had just cut the tape from Sister Evangeline's hands. Sister Evangeline ran to the small altar and removed a linen covering and returned to Joanna, who placed it on the wound and pushed as hard as she could. Michael had managed to walk over to Jennifer and was holding her. She appeared to be in shock.

Martin picked up the phone on the desk and called the rectory. "Grace, bring my black bag to the convent, and hurry."

The front door flew open and two members of the SWAT team ran in. They aimed their guns at Martin. "No!" shouted Michael. "That's Father Martin. Angel is on the floor in the chapel. Call an ambulance. Now!" he commanded. Four more officers entered from the kitchen. "It's over," said Michael.

Jennifer looked at Michael. "I've never shot anyone before," she said softly holding the pistol out in front of her.

"I understand," said Michael gently. He took the gun from her and placed it on the reception desk.

Jennifer noticed that blood was dripping from Michael's fingers. "You've been shot!" she said. The thought of Michael being injured brought her back to the present.

"It's fine," said Michael. "A through and through. Nothing serious. That was a hell of a shot. Right through the habit and from the waist."

"I was just aiming at center mass" she replied. "Is he going to make it?"

As if to answer the question she didn't hear asked, Grace came through the door with Martin's black bag. Martin opened it up and, placing the pall across his shoulders, he returned to Angel and knelt beside him to administer last rites. He anointed his forehead with oil, making the sign of the cross with his thumb, while uttering prayers embedded in his brain. Joanna moved back and sat in a pew. Tears were flowing down her cheeks. Sister Evangeline was attempting to comfort her. "Regardless of what he did, he was our brother," she said.

The paramedics had arrived and were putting Angel on a gurney. Michael recovered his pistol from Angel's pocket. He squeezed Angel's hand and said to him, "Sorry it worked out like this my brother."

Jennifer asked one of the paramedics if he would be okay. "It's unlikely he'll even make it to the hospital ma'am. His vitals are not good. I'm surprised he lasted this long."

Another paramedic was binding the wound in Michael's arm. "You're sure you don't want to go to the hospital Detective?"

"Not right now. I have things to attend to here. I'll drop by the emergency room later, but thank you," Michael said.

The paramedics loaded Angel into the ambulance. Two officers went with him to the hospital. They handcuffed him to the gurney, but it was pretty obvious his killing days were through. They found out later he died on his way to the hospital.

The CSI team arrived and was taping off the entire area, including the house behind the convent. They assured Sister Mary Francis that after they were through in the kitchen and roped off the chapel, the sisters would be free to move throughout the premises. The SWAT team were packing up and preparing to move out, back to their barracks.

Assistant Chief Morrow arrived with the CSI team. He took possession of Jennifer's pistol and explained the procedure for the shooting investigation. He told her she could complete the paperwork on Monday. He assured her that an officer was with Meagan and she was fine. He added that she looked pretty good in the habit. She halfheartedly punched him in the arm.

Martin was on the phone with the Bishop. He reassured him that everybody was all right and that there would be no problem with services on Sunday.

Sister Mary Margaret took Jennifer upstairs to change. Jennifer explained that the habit would be necessary for evidence in the shooting and that the department would reimburse her for a new one. Sister Mary Margaret kept telling her how brave she thought she was. Sister Evangeline came in while she was changing.

"I know you can't appreciate it now, but it's a blessing that it was you and not Michael who fired that shot," Sister Evangeline said softly to Jennifer.

"I don't understand," Jennifer replied.

"Michael is riddled with guilt from his previous assignment. Having killed his own brother might have been too much. I think it would have been too much for him to handle." Sister Evangeline said softly while rubbing Jennifer's shoulders. "You may have saved more lives than you know."

Jennifer turned and hugged Sister Evangeline and finished dressing in silence.

Finally, Michael, Jennifer, Joanna and Martin found themselves alone. They had made their way over to the rectory, where Martin had finally assured Grace that everything was fine and she needed to go home.

"Anyone hungry? I know a place that has plenty of leftovers," Michael said.

"I have to get home to Meagan," Jennifer replied.

"We can stop and pick her up."

"And you should get that arm checked," Jennifer said.

"Tomorrow is soon enough. The paramedics did a fine job. How about it, Joanna? You're not getting out tonight anyway. Martin?"

"Well, I could use a lift to my car. Joanna could come with me and we could pick up some wine and start to warm things up while you get Meagan."

"It's a little too late to include Meagan," Jennifer said. "I'll have Bonnie keep her overnight."

"Sounds like a plan," said Michael. "I guess we have a funeral to plan."

Chapter 49

Saturday morning, Michael woke to the smell of bacon and fresh coffee. His first thought was that Joanna was downstairs making breakfast, but something wasn't right. He looked at the room and was startled. He turned to the other side to look at the pillow next to him. As his mind was clearing and events from the previous night started coming back to him, Jennifer walked in holding a cup of coffee. She was wearing a robe, and from the look of the way it hung on her body, not much else.

"Wake up, sleepy head. I've got breakfast ready and you'll want to take a shower before heading to the hospital to get that bandage changed. Oh, and you need to be out of here before Meagan gets home."

She took a robe out of the closet on the far side of the room and draped it on the foot of the bed. "It was my husband's. I hope you don't mind. I got rid of most of his clothes a long time ago, but for some reason held on to this. Come down and eat and I'll tape that arm off so you can shower afterwards."

Michael started to sit up but winced at the pain in his arm.

"Your pain pills are on the night stand, and I'm sure your arm must hurt. We may have overdone it a little last night." And with that, Jennifer disappeared down the hall.

Michael sat up on the edge of the bed and took two of the Percocet from the bottle on the night stand. As he looked around the room, he saw his clothes scattered around. Other than the pain in his arm, he felt fantastic, if somewhat befuddled. Things were starting to come back to him. It was only meant to be an innocent good night kiss; a simple thank you for a great evening. But Jennifer softly parted her lips and any thoughts about the protocol for comforting a rookie after her first fatal shooting pressed away with the pressure of her body against his. From the doorway to the bedroom was a timed march, and the pain in his arm fell away as gently as their clothes. Jennifer's responses reflected her 6 years of hunger for pleasure other than self driven, and Michael used the pain in his arm to prolong his orgasm till nothing else found space in his mind.

Michael put on the robe from the foot of the bed, picked up his coffee, and headed to the kitchen for breakfast.

"That was quite a performance you put on last night. Much better than the ballet," said Jennifer.

"I'd say it was more of a pas de deux," Michael responded. "You are aware we crossed a line last night?"

"Well, if you can keep that shit-eating grin off your face in the squad room, I think we can get away with it; at least for a while. For someone who was in deep cover for 4 years, it shouldn't be too hard."

Michael flinched at the reference to his past, but Jennifer didn't seem to notice. As Jennifer leaned forward to refill his coffee cup, her robe left just enough room for him to catch a glimpse of the gentle curvature of her breast. He reflected on how delightful her body was.

"Don't even think about it!" Jennifer said. "There isn't time. Meagan will be home in a little over an hour. If you're as good as last night, that isn't nearly enough time."

"When did I give you permission to read my mind?" Michael retorted. "Jen, about last night, I shouldn't have taken advantage of you. You were still in shock from the shooting."

"And here I was thinking that I took advantage of you," she responded. "That was a difficult discussion over dinner last night; watching the three of you dissecting you parent's marriage like that. All blaming each other for the abandonment of Anthony; trying to understand why they made the decisions they did. From the outside listening in it seemed you should have been celebrating a loving home with the usual family problems. How could they go back and turn the past around? You know as well as I do how hard it is to find a child given up for adoption. And what a horrible crisis for your mother to have gone through at such an early age. Your parents found each other again. That's something special. The three of you turned out fine. Oh, look at the time."

Jennifer had Michael take his arm out of the robe and wrapped it in cling wrap. Then she taped the edges with adhesive tape. She couldn't resist brushing against his groin with the back of her hand. When he started to reach for her, she slid away and said, "To the shower for you and don't linger."

Michael feigned a hurt little boy look and headed back to the master bath. As he walked through the bedroom, he picked up his jockey shorts and stepped into the shower.

As the water cascaded over his head, his mind wandered back to his days undercover and his departure from Kate. He tried to let his guilt from betraying her and the gang wash down the drain with the soap running off his body. He knew he couldn't be free until he confronted Kate and at least attempt to explain and, right now, he desperately wanted to close that door. Angel's words kept coming back to him; "We both have things to atone for, isn't that right little brother?" He wished things had worked out better for Angel, and for Kate.

After he was finished with his shower, Michael dressed and joined Jennifer in the kitchen.

"Hey, your car is still at the precinct. I'll come back after I get this thing treated and pick you up to get it."

"Don't worry about it. I feel so good this morning I could almost walk." She gave him a kiss on the cheek. "I'm sure Bonnie will run me down, but don't forget about tomorrow. You, Joanna, Meagan and I are set to attend Martin's service at eleven. We'll be ready by ten. I think it's a terrific way to spend Mother's Day. I hope it's not fire and brimstone, although I can't picture that being Martin's style." She put both hands on Michael's shoulders and gave him a long and loving kiss. "Maybe that's how I'll greet you in the squad room," she said with a laugh.

Michael was totally befuddled on the drive to the hospital. He wasn't at all sure they could pull this off. He finally put it out of his mind with the thought that, worst case scenario, one of them would have to transfer to a different precinct. His mind turned to his plans for after the hospital and the best way to handle that.

In the waiting room of the emergency room, he picked up a copy of the morning paper. A detailed article appeared just below the fold on the front page, with a picture of the convent. The headline read 'Killer taken down in the chapel of St. Anne's Convent'. The article identified the killer as Anthony DeMarko, alias Wallace, nee Davis. Jennifer was listed as the Detective who shot the killer. Michael was mentioned as estranged brother, as was Father Martin Davis. It mentioned that Michael was wounded. Some of Angel's other 'hits' were mentioned as well.

As many times as it had occurred in the past, Michael had never become comfortable with notoriety and this one, with the personal connections, was even more uncomfortable. As if to explain the reason for his discomfort, a nurse came out to lead him to a treatment room and, on the way down the corridor said, "Detective Davis, how horrible for you. It must have been very frightening. Was that Angel person really an unknown brother of yours?"

"Yes. It turned out he was." Michael answered as cordially as possible. "I really can't go into any details till we get it all sorted out. I'm sure you understand."

Luckily the doctor who came in to examine the wound was acquainted with Michael from past injuries. He understood and sent the nurse away. He limited his questions to medical ones, cleaned the hole in his arm and changed his bandage in relative silence. "It's going to take about 3 months to heal completely. Get it checked in about a week. Try not to get the bandages wet. Keep the sling on for a while, but exercise it at least three times a day. I'll give you a script for some mild pain killers. You know the drill."

"Thank you, Doc," Michael said.

"And congratulations on solving the case. As my mother used to say, 'this too shall pass'. Try not to catch any more bullets."

"Will do Doc, and thanks for understanding"

The doctor just smiled. Michael handed in his paperwork, put the script in his pocket and exited the hospital. Once back in his car, he called Joanna to check in. He told her he had something he had to take care of, but should be home by 4 at the latest. She said that she was thawing out some steaks for dinner and that she wanted details over dinner.

It was about 2:00 p.m. as Michael headed over to the South Side. He found a parking spot on a side street off Carson Street, about 2 blocks from a bar he was only too familiar with. As he walked into the bar, he saw Kate leaning on the bar talking to a customer. She obviously spotted him as he walked in but continued talking to her customer. Michael took a seat at the bar and waited. His arm ached from the cleaning, but not nearly as much as his brain. He had gone over this a hundred times in his mind but that all seemed to have been erased. Kate had hardly aged at all. She was pretty, with rough overtones and a killer body. He remembered that she rarely wore makeup, but didn't need it. Her brown hair matched his own and was still long, almost to her waist. He thought about how it used to get tangled with his own as they rolled around the bed in her apartment above the bar.

Kate finished her conversation with a laugh and moved down the bar, settling in front of Michael. "And what can I get for you, Detective?"

Michael was a little taken back by her use of his title. "So you know?"

"Known for quite a while. One of those cops that went down with everybody else ID'd you and told Mitch right after the trial. Within a year everybody knew; whole new definition of dead man walking. Yeah, you screwed all of us royal. What do you want Alex, or should I say Mike?"

"I thought about you a lot Kate. I really cared for you. I hated the way it ended; you thinking of me dead."

"Well, aren't you full of yourself? You did a good job, I'll give you that. Getting stoned, drunk, fighting, roughing dudes up and fucking your way into the group. Mitch says you saved his life once. Don't think he cares about that anymore. Yeah, a real good job."

"I really did care for you Kate. I didn't fake that part. It killed me to leave you like that."

"Obviously didn't kill you enough. If it makes any difference, with all the fucking garbage of the busts, I didn't shed a fucking tear for you. If you came to apologize, don't bother. What you need to do is to start worrying about yourself. George gets out in a couple weeks and another six of the guys get out in a couple months. Mitch don't get out for another 4 but that don't matter. He's running things from the joint. You were a mere pimple on his ass. He's safer locked up if something goes down. I would start sleeping with one eye open if I were you. Now get your fucking ass out of here. I have customers to take care of. I'll give you one thing, you were good in bed but that was all you were good for. I had you replaced before you could rise from the dead. Just get out of here. You're bumming me out."

"Kate…,"Michael started but was cut off by Kate.

"You haven't had enough? Well see how you handle this. I aborted your fucking kid." Michael could see she was starting to tear up. "Now get the hell away from me."

Michael left the bar and made his way back to the car. He got in and just sat there for a good 15 minutes before he could compose himself enough to drive. He finally drove back to his home. It was purely a mechanical function. As he entered the driveway, he could not remember driving home at all. Joanna took one look at him and, without saying a word, led him into the kitchen, opened a beer and had to physically put it into his hand. She waited for him to take a drink.

"Michael, I think you need to tell me what happened."

And so Michael started. He told her about how great the sex was with Jennifer and how great he felt; about their decision to keep it a secret at work but to continue with the relationship; about the hospital and the article in the paper, which she said she had already read; and lastly, he revealed the interchange with Kate.

"Oh, Michael," Joanna said. She could see the decimating effect the interchange had had on Michael. "She may have just made that up to upset you. She seems vindictive enough. She just wanted to hurt you."

"I don't think so. She was on the verge of breaking down."

"Michael, I'm going to cook dinner. You'll feel better after you eat. This too shall pass."

"That's what the doctor said."

"The doctor? Did you go back to the hospital?"

"No. He said it earlier while treating my arm. Why do people say that? It's a lie. Some things just don't pass."

They ate in relative silence and Michael decided he'd had enough for one day.

"Sorry sis, I'm not much company tonight. I think I'm just going to turn in."

That's fine, Michael. I'll clean up the kitchen and then watch TV. I want to see what the news has to say. Remember, we're going to mass tomorrow. Will Jennifer and Meagan be joining us?"

The thought of seeing Jennifer lifted his spirits a bit. "Yes, I'm picking them up at 10."

"Well, try and get some sleep. See you in the morning."

Chapter 50

Michael felt quite a bit better when he woke up Sunday morning. He dressed and went down to the kitchen where Joanna was already making breakfast.

"If you stay here any longer I'm going to gain weight," Michael said. "Oh, Happy Mother's Day." For a brief moment, the idea of Mother's Day brought Kate to mind, but he fought it off. "Do you think I need a tie? It's been a long time since I've been to mass."

"You're asking me? I'm a Protestant. We don't wear ties."

"Good, I'll be Protestant for the day."

"But Jennifer's Episcopal. I think they wear ties."

The thought of Jennifer and Meagan once again raised his spirits.

"Damn. I enjoyed being Protestant. Oh well, a tie it is."

"I think they're all just happy to see people coming through the doors nowadays," Joanna said. "Make sure you have some small bills for the collection plate."

"Yeah, with Angel gone, they're going to need all the collections they can get," Michael replied.

Joanna and Michael pulled into Jennifer's driveway at 10 on the dot. Meagan ran out and gave Michael a big hug. She was wearing a dress and her new heels from the ballet. She looked adorable. Michael's glance turned to Jennifer coming down the front steps. She was wearing a very tasteful dress and wearing a hat. She had another hat in her hand for Meagan.

Michael greeted her with a kiss. "Well, that will go over well in the squad room," Jennifer said with a smile. Meagan also caught it and had a big smile.

"Happy Mother's Day," Michael said. He was blushing at his enthusiasm. Kate had left his mind entirely.

They shared idle talk on their way to St. Anne's. Meagan was excited about a boy she had met at a dance a on Saturday. He was a sophomore! That started a conversation about dating and appropriate behavior. Jennifer took the lead and carefully explained about boys and the need for caution. Michael had trouble keeping from laughing. The irony was not missed by Jennifer either.

They arrived at the church and were greeted at the door by Martin. They exchanged pleasantries, went in, and found a seat in the fourth pew from the front. Joanna said they were much more comfortable when your hands and feet were not taped up. Meagan looked puzzled by that but let it slide.

Soon the service started. Martin had made some changes to the normal liturgy for the day. The first reading was the tale of the Prodigal Son and the second was The Good Shepherd. When it was time for the Gospel, he read the prescribed Gospel for the day and then, after everybody was seated, began his sermon. He started by recognizing that most of those present had heard by now of the events of this past Friday. He briefly retold the story of the kidnapping of the sisters, his personal sister and himself. He left out the actual shooting, but acknowledged that the person who committed these deeds was in fact a brother that none of them had known about. He continued by stating that there could be no more appropriate day to address the difficulty some women find themselves in then Mother's Day, and how terrible it must be to deal with the choices that face those who find themselves forced with making those choices. He restated the church's position on sex before marriage and abortion, but acknowledged that not all faiths treated these the same way and indeed, the flesh is weak and people within the church also find themselves in these conditions.

At this point in the sermon, he explained he had changed the readings for the day to help us understand how he believed God treated these souls. His belated brother was the prodigal son who had wasted his life and the gifts that his Father had given him but was welcomed back into family, albeit posthumously. He explained that his mother had put her son up for adoption with the best of intentions, but the world had driven him to a different path. To the Lord they were sheep who had been lost to the flock, but meant so much to the Lord that he sought to bring them back. They both, in their own way, had sought atonement for their indiscretions. He explained that he had performed Last Rites for his brother. Now it is for the Lord to judge the value of their lives and hopefully rejoin His flock. He invited the congregation to pray for them that they may feel the forgiveness that He offers those that atone for their sins.

As the congregation stood to pray at the end of the sermon, Jennifer took Michael's hand and gave it a squeeze. His mind instantly cleared of his doubts and fears. At that moment, he felt absolved.

About the same time as Kate was relaying a story to George in the visitor room of a state prison.